CONFLICT
OF
LOYALTIES

RELIGION AND CIVILIZATION SERIES

THE COMMUNICATION OF IDEAS
Lyman Bryson, *Editor*

RELIGION AND THE WORLD ORDER

WORLD ORDER: ITS INTELLECTUAL AND CULTURAL FOUNDATIONS

FOUNDATIONS OF DEMOCRACY

WELLSPRINGS OF THE AMERICAN SPIRIT

F. Ernest Johnson, *Editor*

GROUP RELATIONS AND GROUP ANTAGONISMS

CIVILIZATION AND GROUP RELATIONSHIPS

UNITY AND DIFFERENCE IN AMERICAN LIFE

DISCRIMINATION AND NATIONAL WELFARE

GREAT EXPRESSIONS OF HUMAN RIGHTS
R. M. MacIver, *Editor*

LABOR'S RELATION TO CHURCH AND COMMUNITY
Liston Pope, *Editor*

GENERAL EDITORIAL BOARD

Louis Finkelstein
F. Ernest Johnson   R. M. MacIver
George N. Shuster

*Institute for Religious and Social Studies,
Jewish Theological Seminary of America*

RELIGION AND CIVILIZATION SERIES

CONFLICT
OF
LOYALTIES

A series of addresses and discussions

EDITED BY

R. M. MacIver

LIEBER PROFESSOR EMERITUS OF POLITICAL PHILOSOPHY
AND SOCIOLOGY, COLUMBIA UNIVERSITY

Published by

The INSTITUTE for RELIGIOUS and SOCIAL STUDIES

Distributed by

HARPER & BROTHERS

NEW YORK AND LONDON

**Discarded by
Dartmouth College Library**

COPYRIGHT, 1952
BY THE INSTITUTE FOR RELIGIOUS AND SOCIAL STUDIES

*All rights reserved including the right
of reproduction in whole or in part
in any form.*

PRINTED IN THE UNITED STATES OF AMERICA
BY THE VAIL-BALLOU PRESS, INC., BINGHAMTON, N. Y.

This volume is based on lectures given at The Institute for Religious and Social Studies of The Jewish Theological Seminary of America during the winter of 1950–1951. Doctor Alexander Sachs was to have contributed to both the series and the volume, but unfortunately was prevented from doing so.

Each chapter in this volume represents solely the individual opinion of the author. Neither the Institute nor the editor assumes responsibility for the views expressed. The contributors were invited to address the Institute because of the special contribution each could make to general knowledge of the subject.

CONTENTS

BY WAY OF INTRODUCTION

An Ancient Tale Retold   *R. M. MacIver*   1

THE RULE VERSUS THE CAUSE

I. On Deceiving the Public for the Public Good
   Lyman Bryson   9

II. Fact, Fiction, and Reality   *F. Ernest Johnson*   25

III. On the Justifiable Grounds of Disobedience to Law
   Roger N. Baldwin   37

IV. On the Limits of Justifiable Disobedience
   Franz L. Neumann   45

V. On the Enlistment of Dubious Allies   *Hans Simons*   57

VI. On "Making Friends with the Mammon of Unrighteousness"   *Liston Pope*   69

SOME CONFLICTS OF OUR TIMES

VII. The Hiroshima Issue   *W. W. Waymack*   77

VIII. Institutionalism and the Faith   *Louis Finkelstein*   89

IX. Freedom and Interference in American Education
   Ordway Tead   99

X. Private Profit and Public Interest in Mass Communication
   Robert Saudek   113

XI. The Threat to Privacy   *Harold D. Lasswell*   121

Contributors to "Conflict of Loyalties"   141

Index   143

CONFLICT
OF
LOYALTIES

BY WAY OF INTRODUCTION: AN ANCIENT TALE RETOLD

BY

R. M. MacIVER

Ever since human beings set up organizations they have been beset by the problem of clashing loyalties. In early times the conflict arose chiefly between the demand of the state and the contrary demand of the faith or of the kin. Already there were two or more loyalties, and sometimes they could not be reconciled. Aristotle, who probed into so many things, remarked that it was perhaps not the same thing to be a good *man* and to be a good *citizen*. But long before Aristotle the conflict had stimulated the poet philosophers of Greece. It was a favorite theme of Greek tragedy—indeed it is the chief theme of all the great tragedies of all peoples. The Greeks took the theme from the heroic legends in which it first found expression. In the starkest form it animates the tragedy of Orestes and the tragedy of Oedipus. But it was the burden of many another tale, and one of these is the subject of our discussion here.

Think over the great dramas of all times, and you will find that they concentrate on the issue of clashing loyalties. Begin with what is perhaps the greatest of all plays, Hamlet, and the same theme provokes the poet to his profoundest reflections. The hero, the vacillating prince, is bidden by the insistent and horror-fed demands of a prime loyalty to do an act that violates his whole attachment to the ordered ways of life. He shrinks but cannot evade the choice, and his shrinking only brings in the end a greater cumulation of tragedy.

From these old themes I choose the story of Antigone, because it has been discussed by various philosophers some of whom have declared that Antigone chose aright, and others of whom have said she made the wrong choice, while one philosopher, with his usual Olympic indifference to the conditions under which men must live and act, proclaimed that she was both wrong and right![1] But the reader must decide for himself after he has heard the story.

Antigone is the daughter of Oedipus, King of Thebes, most renowned of all tragic figures. When Oedipus is gone, his two sons take over Thebes as rulers, but one of them drives out the other and becomes the sole ruler of the city. One was named Eteocles, and the other Polynices. Eteocles drove out his brother from greed of power.

Polynices, now exiled, gets together an alien army at the city of Argos. This army invades the home city of Thebes. The enemy is outside the walls. There is much hand to hand conflict, as was common in the old Greek warfare, and in this conflict the two brothers meet and kill one another. Thereupon another member of the family, whose name is Creon, takes command. The besiegers are defeated; the city is again safe and free.

The first thing that Creon, the new king, does is to issue an edict. This edict provides for an honorable burial for the hero, Eteocles, and it brings down denunciation and disgrace upon the other brother, the traitor. The body of the invader lies outside the walls of the city and the king proclaims that it must not be given the customary burial rites. It must lie outside the walls for the birds and beasts. The traitor must be dishonored in every way possible and Creon vows dire punishment on anyone who disobeys his edict.

Here is where Antigone enters. Antigone is not only the sister of the "traitor" who lies outside the walls, she is also the niece of King Creon. She feels the strong pull of the kin-bond because, according to the rites of their religion, the nearest of kin must pay burial dues to the dead. It is a most sacred obligation. It is sacred in two senses—first, because it is the law of the kin, and, second, because it is for her the law of God.

Antigone is forbidden by her king to perform this sacred function, these last rites. What shall she do? Shall she obey her king or shall she obey her religion and be true to her kin? She decides that the sacred obligation to the kin comes first. She goes outside the walls

[1] Hegel, in his *Philosophy of Religion*.

By Way of Introduction: An Ancient Tale Retold

and sprinkles a handful of dust on the body. That is all that is necessary. It is a symbolic thing. The sprinkling of dust suffices. She is discovered. She is brought before the king. The king is incensed. In his fury he condemns her to a terrible death. She pleads with him, but he declares that to show any sympathy, any mercy, any consideration for a traitor, is to destroy the very foundations of all law and order. It is to destroy the state. The first duty of every citizen is to insure that law abides.

If one in any way condones treason, then he is shaking the very edifice on which everything is built. Such is the argument of the king. Antigone is led away. Presently the lover of Antigone appears. To make things still more perplexed in this tangle of clashing loyalties, he is the son of King Creon. He, very soberly, very quietly, and very earnestly, pleads again with the king. He puts before the king what his duty is to religion, to his gods, and what will happen if he flouts the divine command.

However, the king again asserts his position. He, above all, must uphold the law. He will never permit anyone who has been a traitor to escape the penalty. So, the lover, the son of the king and the lover of Antigone, at last yields, goes out with the intent that he will not survive his beloved one. But he does not move the king.

Antigone is condemned to be immured in a rocky prison to die a slow, lingering death there. She is led away. The chorus of the play, composed of Theban elders, now sings a song of the triumph of love. It begins:

O Love, unconquered in battle, you make havoc of possessions, you keep your vigil on the soft cheek of a maiden; none can escape you, neither the immortal gods nor man whose life is for a day. And he whom you visit is beside himself.

Then, in the play, at the last moment, the ancient prophet of the people comes before the king. He is terribly concerned. Dreadful signs are happening. The omens are threatening. All things portend catastrophes for Thebes, and it is because the king has flouted the will of the gods.

To this last argument the king very reluctantly and finally yields.

He decides that perhaps he went too far. So, to avert this doom, he will go and see that the slain traitor is given at least some kind of burial. He dare not disobey the manifested will of the gods; he will go and liberate Antigone, to avoid the wrath of Heaven.

He arrives at the rocky tomb where Antigone is imprisoned. Antigone, faced with the prospect of this long, lingering death, sealed up in these walls, has taken her veil and hanged herself. The king and his company come and witness the scene. In the company is Antigone's lover and the young man in madness rushes at the king, threatening him. The king escapes and then the lover kills himself with the sword with which he threatened the king.

There the play ends. But the last word, spoken as usual by the chorus, is as follows: "Wisdom is the greatest of things and reverence to the gods should be inviolate."

The story of Antigone is one that philosophers have discussed right through from the time of Plato to the present. They have taken different positions concerning whether Antigone did right or wrong. Should she have chosen that way? Should she not?

Antigone, as everybody admits, was faced with a terrible decision whichever way she chose. Some read one lesson in the play as presented by Sophocles; some another. The king, some say, was wrong because he overstepped the divine law. In his desire for revenge, he proceeded too far and paid no attention to the sanctities or the obligations of kinship. Antigone, some say, was wrong because she was not in the position of king and she as a citizen was bound to obey. Others point out that the whole tenor of the play is to arouse our feelings in favor of Antigone. And the words with which it closed, "reverence to the gods should be inviolate," some understand to mean that the playwright accepted the argument of Antigone.

Finally, there is the position of Hegel that "In the light of eternal justice, Antigone was both right and wrong." And so was Creon.

May I be excused if I find this ineffable impartiality very unpleasant—and not least when the philosopher in question professes to speak "in the light of eternal justice."

Commentators are still arguing the ancient question. The *Political Science Quarterly* some time back contained two articles by John

Dickinson on the theory of sovereignty, in one of which the author condemned Antigone for making the wrong decision. He contrasted what he called the "primitive attitude" of Antigone with the "mature comprehension" of Socrates.

Socrates had been in what looked like a somewhat similar position. But it really was different. Socrates was condemned to death, unjustly as he believed, and as everybody who knew him believed. When at the last moment some of his friends contrived to visit him in prison and provide him with means of escape, so that the way was open for him to escape from Athens, Socrates refused to move. He said, "No. How can I? Here I am now an old man. I have lived in this city all my life, and the laws of this city have established all my ways. Without them none of us could live. These laws, these codes under which we live, I have accepted them throughout my life. They brought me into the world. They educated me. I owe everything to them. We cannot say in turn, if they dishonor us, if they even at times treat us as we know we should not be treated, even if they condemn us to death, we have no right to turn back and say, 'In return we will violate you.' They have a greater claim on us than we have on them."

So Plato put the case in the name of Socrates. I am not at all sure that Socrates himself had these ideas, but Plato wrote the dialogue called *Crito* in which he represented Socrates as arguing thus against his friends. John Dickinson, accordingly, contrasts the behavior of Socrates who refused to disobey the law even to save his life, even though he was falsely condemned, with the attitude of Antigone who felt that she could take it to her own conscience to say whether or not she should obey.

Dickinson used the same argument that King Creon used—the law is first and paramount. If we break the law deliberately, if we deliberately defy it, then we are voting for the dissolution of society, as it were. We are then denying the foundations on which all our order, all our stability, all our peace, all the conditions under which we live, everything we have, depend.

There is, however, some confusion in this argument. More than one kind of law is necessary to hold a society together. Custom, too, is a bond of society, and surely the moral law is also, and the faith by which men live, and the conscience that animates all loyalties. What we call "the law of the land" would not be very strong if it were not also for custom, and custom would not be strong unless there was also a thing called conscience. There are many ties that bind men, not one alone. The legal code is a very essential, a primary one, but it is not the only one. It is not the only foundation of social order. As Dickinson himself put it elsewhere, there is a "law behind law." The problem of Antigone is one we all have, in our own way, to meet. We are not in the position of a king or a princess, or somebody else who has to make this decision in high places, but every one of us sometime or other must choose between conflicting values and conflicting codes.

For example, if you are a doctor, you have sometimes to decide which of two loyalties you should obey. If you are a lawyer, it comes to you in another form; if you are a clergyman it comes in yet another form. Everyone, according to his responsibilities and his relationships, must at some moment choose which code to obey and which to violate.

I remember I was once discussing the political doctrine of Machiavelli with a class of students. Machiavelli, as you know, shocked the world, because he said that rulers should not try to be ethical if it did not pay them; their first duty was to keep things secure and if they had to go against humanity and cheat and deceive and break their promises, if that were the only way they could make the state secure, then they should do just that.

So I asked first what was to be said in favor of Machiavelli. To bring home the point I raised the question about what they, the members of this group, would do under certain conditions. Would they be willing to tell a lie deliberately, and justify it? Was it ever *right* to tell a lie? That was the issue—whether it was right.

I took various hypothetical cases, after which the minority who had said "no," yielded—all but one member. I was not trying to convert them to anything. I was trying to find out what they really thought and I took certain cases, including one that concerned a doctor and his patient.

When I finished, one student alone took the complete negative— "No, it is never right." I did not seek to discredit the viewpoint anyone really had. I was about to leave the matter there when one of my students said, "May I tell a personal story?" This was his story. "I was born in Vienna. When I was thirteen years old, my father was very ill and the doctor was called in. I saw the doctor as he left my father's room and I said to him, 'How is he?' He answered, 'Your father does not have long to live.' I said, 'Doctor, please do not tell that to my mother, I beg you!' The doctor replied: 'We had better prepare her for it. I shall tell her the truth.'

"That was seventeen years ago," the student said, "and my mother died in a week of the shock. My father is still alive." I did not draw any moral. I do not know what the moral is, but you see now the kind of problems we are going to face in this volume, problems where the codes clash, problems where we have to choose between loyalties, problems where we have to get beyond the rules to our final values.

There is, I believe, a way of looking clearly, sensibly, and rightly at these problems. Let us seek it for ourselves as we proceed.

I

ON DECEIVING THE PUBLIC FOR THE PUBLIC GOOD

BY

LYMAN BRYSON

This boldly stated question, "Should a leader deceive the public for the public good?" is not likely to get less important as time goes on, for leaders do not get less powerful or less ambitious and the means of deceiving the people increases. We have made political leaders more than ever dependent on the suffrage of their followers, but we have put mechanical messengers into their hands by which they can coerce public consent. The growth of an industrial culture has tended also to enlarge constantly the units of organization in which men work, and also the collectives in which they think and communicate with each other and act together. The great collectives take over more and more of our lives, in their economic and political aspects especially, and make it more and more difficult for us to see the relations between what we do and any general principles of truth or rightness. The leader is tempted by the tools of manipulation. Is it ever wise for him to use them?

We ought first to ask ourselves the more general question: What are leaders for? Why do we need leaders in a free country? I would answer that the leader's function is to help to determine, in any crisis, which of our possible selves will act. We are all multiple: our personalities are bundles of possible responses, each with the accent of our own peculiar self, but still all widely differing from each other. If we could always be counted on, each one of us, always to act in the same way, no matter how we are challenged, life and politics would be much simpler. It would also be dull and uninteresting: our unpredictability is part of our human charm. The leader is an embodied suggestion, and the combinations of causes and chances that determine the leader who will catch our attention and our support at any time, are the causal chain of history.

We might suppose, for an example, that the people of a tragically unhappy country like Germany could have followed a more calm and righteous leader than Hitler, and that they had all reacted to the pressure of the situation in the same way. In that case there might never have been a world conflict. We know that the Germans were confused, as well as hurt. Some of them, as we know from the investigations of Theodore Abel and other sociologists, tried to retreat into a fantasy of martyrdom. To them the world was not only tragic; it was unjust. They could blame anyone but themselves for what had happened. Others took refuge in crime, as if to say, "Since all the foundations of our state have been destroyed, we'll get what we can for ourselves out of the wreck." Others were willing to begin the hard work of reconstruction. And among the possibilities was the idea of reasserting the greatness of the German people and the German state. It was possible to believe that Germany was still one of the strong and aggressive factors in the world. All these possible ways of reacting existed among the German people, and many of them existed side by side within the personalities of every individual German. Each man or woman was more or less capable of making any one of these responses to trouble, and the one the great mass took was what was suggested by the most persuasive leadership.

What did Hitler actually do? He called out the aggressive self that was latent in practically every normal German and made it the dominant active self. He made most of them as aggressive as they were individually capable of being. More than that, he called out and got into positions of power all the Germans who were even more than normally aggressive, and the nation was put in a generally aggressive and dangerous posture. Great crises make for great instability of selves, or of character, and Germany's crisis was catastrophic. The result was an enormous overdevelopment of a normal human trait, socially organized and expressed. This, in generally less damaging ways, sometimes to our great good, is the function of the leader. He cannot make

On Deceiving the Public for the Public Good

us over; he can make us be our best or our worst within our range.

A free country, which is our ideal and our partial accomplishment, has the same need for leaders of the right kind as any other. But before we conclude this discussion we have to ask ourselves another question of general principle. What is the purpose of political life and active citizenship in a free country? I believe that the purpose of sharing in the political thought of my country, and of my own community as a part of it, is not ultimately the solution of political problems. Freedom for men to think and learn and act on their acquired wisdom is, I believe, more likely to get good solutions for political problems than any other system; our record would prove that. But even if there were a better way of getting the merely correct technical, or practical —shall we say, the material answers?—to a political problem, I would still hold fast to democracy and to decision by the people. Our ultimate judgment on a social or a political system should not be based, solely, on the criterion of practical success. It is based on the evidence of growth in the people. Sometimes free men make mistakes; they must be allowed that privilege. If they learn the lessons of politics and conduct from making mistakes, the principle of democracy is fulfilled. Whether or not there are other areas of living, outside the political, in which this principle cannot be followed, is another question. We shall stick to politics.

I can turn to Germany again for an example to make the point. Several years ago a small group of German women who were then holding political office at home were brought over here for some lessons in American ideas of democracy. Asked to help in that project, I chose to meet them after they had made their journeys and observations. I wanted to hear their questions, after they knew what America looked like. In the conversation we had, one of the most intelligent of the nine women struggled to understand the essential relation in a democracy between freedom and authority, political freedom and technical authority. She told of being in a city where the administration of municipal affairs was entrusted to a city manager. He was appointed because of his professional competence and experience. He was an excellent person and it was evident that he would know the right answers to most practical questions. And yet—this disturbed her deeply—the members of the city council, who were not elected for professional competence, had final authority to overrule his decisions. Even his right decisions! she said.

My answer was that the principle of democracy would always make it necessary for the directly elected representatives of the people to have the final word. Even when they were wrong? Even when, by any technical judgment, they were wrong. And I insisted that she would not understand democracy until she could see why that had to be so. I tried to explain to her that she was still thinking of political action as having no purpose other than to solve political problems, and that if this principle, which was ultimately not democratic but authoritarian, was followed in any country, the rule of the people would eventually be ended. The purpose of political action and the opportunity of free political life is for the people ultimately to determine their own destiny, and—after they have had the chance to learn—even to make their own mistakes. The great end they are serving is the development of their country through the development of themselves, not by authoritative interventions, no matter how competent or benevolent. It is not true that tyrants can never be benevolent. The trouble is that they go on being tyrants, and under tyranny individual men dry up for lack of spiritual exercise.

We too often forget that it means something real and important, and perhaps greatly daring, to say that the purpose of a democratic society is to make great persons, that the end is the development of the person by experience and not the technical answers to civic problems. In fact, political experience has been and still is, and probably will always be, one of the greatest of the educational factors in any person's life; it cannot count for much unless it includes free decisions and a chance to learn from the consequences. We have to decide for ourselves in the light of what we can learn of the facts, and then learn the great lessons from the results of our choice. Both collective organization and authority can interfere with this purpose and defeat us. Unless we learn from politics, then politics is not worth our time. Decisions should be made for the good of the state, but the ultimate value of all political decisions is the experience of bearing part of the responsibility of making them.

The leader, then, is a person who helps us to choose, and if he is a great leader he helps us also to learn. He cannot do his work for us, if this is what we demand of him, in any society where the closed theories of freedom prevail. Through the long course of political and social debate in Western history there have been two ideas of freedom, and this is not the place to question the sincerity of those who take the ancient line that we, in America, have learned to reject. The closed theory of freedom, as it is advocated vigorously in all totalitarian countries, is that men have a right to know an official doctrine which is always called the truth. But it implies also that they have a right to know nothing but this official doctrine, and that the state or some other authoritative group of men, acting in the name of the doctrine embodied in some institution, have the right to interfere in their experience and keep them from knowing anything contrary to it. It implies that authority, which in considering our problem, means the men in power, knows what the truth is, and will keep all citizens of the state from any contamination with any other opinion. This is called "freedom" in totalitarian countries, and its defenders can look for support to a long line of teachers in our Western tradition. The other theory, the open theory, which has an equally numerous body of teachers behind it and is the dominant ideal of freedom for which we have fought for centuries, and which we have attempted to embody in our American political institutions, is that men must seek truth by free choice and consequence. They must have the freedom to make mistakes, because freedom is given for the ultimate purpose of democratic political life which is individual growth.

These are all preliminary considerations which must be taken into account, I think, before we can answer our question: which is, if you have forgotten, "Should a leader deceive the public for the public good?" But we still have to answer another prior question: "What kind of society do we want?" There seems to be good evidence in history and in our own times that only those societies that believe their own political slogans and in the myths of their national virtue can build successful empires. By this, I mean, of course, that nations which dominate others must first put themselves under spiritual domination.

This is not the same thing as to say that we should lose our democracy if we set out to run the world; I do not believe that the problem is best put in those terms. Certainly other nations in the remote past and in approximately modern times have built empires and still remained democracies. Britain is the best example; Britain built her empire and her own democracy through the same period. But it is still true that nations which set out more or less deliberately to dominate other nations must be ruled by men who pronounce some political slogans that are not to be questioned, and if the people have even a healthy skepticism toward the goals of empire or the myths of their country's unspecked virtue, the will to power is fatally weakened.

We need only look at the difference between the attitude of the Greeks, who brilliantly failed at empire, and the attitude of the Romans who brilliantly succeeded. It is not now a question of their degrees of democracy at home, although we might have stopped to notice that Rome also built her empire while building her civil law and the civil rights of her people. The point is to mark the difference between a magnificently endowed but skeptical people like the Greeks, and a very different people, the Romans, who learned how to conquer. We can be quite sure, I think, that most of the Romans who brought their own version of the classical civilization to the Western world and gave the Mediterranean basin several centuries of magnificent peace, really believed that Roman ideas and Roman slogans were not only best but were not to be examined. The Greeks in their most insolent moments never seemed able quite to believe that their imperial depredations were for the good of subjected peoples. When the Romans began their career as a mean tribe with great ideas, in the little group of hills in the center of Italy, when they conquered and took more and more of their neighbors into the Roman state, they believed not only that it was good for the Romans but also good for the slaves and the conquered who might, of course, end up by being taken into citizenship but who were, in the meantime, to be made over in the Roman image. They believed their slogans and took over the Western world.

It helps to have the slogans and the political myths founded on facts,

On Deceiving the Public for the Public Good

but the crucial point is that they are believed. Today we can study the British and find them much like the Romans in their early brutal innocence and faith, like them also perhaps in the late phase, their present refinement, their discovery that social welfare at home is more important than carrying the white man's burden, perhaps that the white man's burden can be best carried at home, their period of the Antonines. We can, if necessary, save them from the next stage of being overcome by barbarians. But when they were powerful, they were extraordinary for efficiency as rulers and for self-confidence. They believed their own stuff. The French, on the other hand, like the Greeks, have long since been skeptical and weak imperialists. The principle holds.

We do not know how much of our own destiny is ever in our own hands. This is a philosophic, not a practical, question we are dealing with and we can assume for ourselves the power of national choice. We do not need to destroy our own freedoms to save us from destroying the freedoms of others; that ironic crime has often been committed, to keep freedom at home and conquer abroad. Witness Britain and India. The cost of empire lies not in our political freedoms, but in the adjacent area of our freedom to know and to learn by free informed experience. To lead us into building an empire, provided it is possible to us in material terms, our leaders have got to convince us and keep us convinced that all slogans of imperialism are true, that we are destined because of our virtue as well as our strength to subdue the world for its own sake, to spread the unquestioned doctrines of our own political and economic commonplaces, to repeat again the sorry old pattern of dominion.

The purpose of empire building, however, is not the building of great citizens; it is the building of a great state. Great states are built by leaders who lead their people into sacrifice for dreams of power and glory, who lead them to believe that some kinds of doctrinally prescribed freedom may be good for them but that weaker peoples must be led. Great men and women are built by leaders who lead them into sacrifice for the right freely to seek the truth.

It has to be made quite clear, I believe, that a love of free inquiry and other higher virtues will not destroy the power of a great nation, nor make it helpless against attack, by force or by insidious ideas. It is altogether likely that, in modern circumstances, an open freedom of thought will make a country materially strong, as well as strong in spirit. There is as yet no evidence whatever that totalitarian countries, which suppress skepticism and honest deviation in the name of doctrine, or officially pronounced "truth," can either build or manage a really great industrial system which depends in the long run on the freedom of skill and invention. Neither Britain nor Germany nor the United States created a great industrial state by totalitarian management. Russia has not yet proved that it can succeed industrially after thirty-three years of effort. Our point, however, lies elsewhere. What we are saying is that great citizens can be built only when leaders will dare to let them use their own minds, when the state helps us to knowledge of alternative choices, conserving for us the essential democratic experience, which is to seek the truth by our own efforts, to know it as far as it can be known, to act on it freely, and to learn freely from free action. We can be strong and we can be free. If we want to dominate others and shove our doctrines down the throats of weaker peoples, then our leaders will have to deal often in lies in order to blind us to the true picture of our behavior.

This question, then, can be put in Kantian terms. We can follow Immanuel Kant's distinction: we can take men as means or as ends. It is as simple and as difficult as that. If men are to be used as means, if human beings are to be treated by their leaders as means to an end —and I am specifying nothing whatever as to the quality or character of that end, even the realization of national power, or the greatness of an institution, the realization of an ideal, or the sacrifice of the present to the future—if men are to be taken as means to an end, then it is inevitable that leaders will at certain times deceive them for the public good. But if we accept Kant's ethical principle and believe that men should never be used as means but always as ends in themselves, if their experience is the purpose of political life, then the leader, by interfering with the people's experience of free inquiry, no matter how bitter their discoveries may be, is defeating democracy.

The distinction is easy but to make it work is difficult, because a leader, even within my definition, is always also a teacher. Part of his job in every situation and on any scale of operation, social or political or intellectual, is to enlarge constantly the range of thought and the range of possible choices in the minds of his followers. A leader who believes in our kind of democracy, which we practice with considerable success, although we often get mixed up in trying to define it, will say, "My duty is also the duty of a teacher, to increase men's freedom by enlarging their knowledge." The biggest dimension of freedom is the dimension of knowing. As we have to repeat, over and over in these days of deliberate obfuscation and innocent confusions, the choice you never can make is the choice you never heard of. Ignorance is not only a chain on your mind, it is also a chain that binds your will.

Any kind of so-called freedom that protects men against making mistakes cannot be what we are talking about, because you cannot protect men from error except by protecting them against knowledge. Any government or institution or leader that sets out to protect men from making mistakes must act on the assumption that there is an ultimate truth that can be stated as final closed doctrine—and here I am still speaking of political and social truths because religious truth may present other problems—not only that there is an ultimate truth but that it can be exactly stated and that they can state it better than anyone else. It implies that this doctrine is of a kind that cannot maintain itself by its own character in the open market of ideas, and that it cannot do its work for men unless they are forcibly prevented from ever hearing anything else.

This is the principle, explicitly stated in their own documents, followed by the present Russian government. The Russians argue in international committees: "We have freedom of information in Russia because all agencies of information are in the hands of the government and therefore they cannot fall into the hands of anyone who would deceive the people." In spite of the fact that such a statement seems to us either naive or cynical, as it does not admit the ever present danger that the government might be the agency that was out to fool the people, we must take it, I think, as sincere. It is in the minds of sincere persons that it can really do the most damage. We need not really fear very much those who are cynical enough to realize that they are using suppression of knowledge to keep themselves in power and laugh with each other behind closed conference doors. Institutions founded on cynicism have a way of disintegrating. It is possible, of course, for men in the Kremlin to think this is a joke, although I doubt even that. It is absolutely necessary, if Russia is to last very long as a totalitarian state, that the rank and file of the bureaucracy, the little leaders, believe in what they are doing.

No, the most dangerous tyrant is the one who has succumbed to the ultimate corruption of power and believes in his own benevolence. He can believe that he is helping the people, that he is doing us good by keeping us from knowing anything but the official doctrine whatever it may be. He will in all honesty and zeal keep us from learning by our own choice.

You may be thinking that we do not learn much from experience and that making a mistake is not a step that leads always to wisdom. This is true enough; if we learned from our mistakes and never repeated them, the world would not be so full of defeated and frustrated people. But, however much we may fail to learn from experience, it is quite certain that there are many things we cannot learn from anything else. They cannot be handed down to us, nor handed out, and if there is any new truth in the world it will not be discovered by men who are protected from error.

So we come back again to the leader. His chief work is to help us make a choice. He can lead us to take great spiritual risks and be great citizens. Or, he can play safe, stick to the doctrine, and let us drift into the fallacies of power. In that case, we may possibly win an empire but we are almost certain to lose our own souls. I am making a clear contrast here, between greatness in nations and greatness in men, meaning power and domination on the one hand, and the expansion of the soul by the search for truth, on the other. These are different ideals, and it often happens in the practical affairs of men that nations attain to mixtures and combinations of the ideals that are held by various members of their national group. By my own preference among the definitions of freedom, I should have to say that I should prefer a nation in which there was a generous variety of different goals, on all levels of political opinion, except in those matters that would endanger freedom itself. And I do not believe that all the overt national actions of a national group will always serve the same ideal. What we are seeking is the answer to a question that proposes a choice between two kinds of effort and two kinds of demand to be made on our leaders, knowing that the results will be mixed. The true spirit of freedom and power are not antithetical, any more than righteousness and prosperity are antitheses. But the man who seeks prosperity above righteousness will probably lose both, and the nation that seeks power above truth will have the same double disaster.

The alternative that we are not quite willing to state in realistic terms can be put this way: Do we want our leaders to decide what shall be our national fate without letting us in on their secret, and then manipulate our ignorance to achieve what they think we ought to have, without our knowing what are the other choices? It might be said that a little license to a ruler is not a mandate for tyranny. The difficulty is that if we give willingly to a leader the right to deceive us, we give over to him also the right and the chance to decide when and whenever the deceit shall be practiced. It is certain that the fates of nations are mixed, evil with good, and we may seek virtue even while we have a concern for material power. But which value is to be sacrificed to the other? It is the habit of knowing what value is to be held to, even at the cost of the others, that gives us our national morality.

In the present crisis in American life, it is important to look closely at one assumption, an almost unconscious assumption that gets into much discussion of our possible future power and influence. It is taken for granted and it is false. The notion, which you will meet in all kinds of writing and talk and political polemics, is that we can justify our material power, even a career of material domination, by the cultural achievements that our power makes possible. I mean, of course, cultural achievements by ourselves, great art and thought and science and philosophy, the great expression of our own ideals. And the notion is false because, in spite of the commonplaces of the textbooks and careless historians, great cultural achievements have not been inevitably, or even generally, concurrent with great material power, and certainly are not the results of it.

This is a thesis that shocks certain kinds of commonplace minds because the fallacy is so comforting. It may be selfish of us to spread over the world, by the means of bayonets and bombs. But we bring civilization and much more; we express our own greatness for the good of later generations in imperishable art and thought. Look at Periclean Greece, and Elizabethan England and France under Louis XIV and the others. Well, I ask you really to look at them. This is no place for a thoroughgoing analysis of the relations, at these times, of the factors of power and cultural productiveness, but I am saying as boldly as I know how that the idea that nations grow great materially and then, and as a result, show greatness in art and thought and in letters, is a fallacy, unhistorical, and untrue.

If the fate of any nation displayed before our contemporary eyes were needed to set up the truth of the relation between material power and cultural achievement, it could well be found in Germany. Between Bismarck and Hitler, Germany dominated Europe and made two bids toward world hegemony that terrified and exhausted the rest of Europe. Out of that time, whose names will be remembered with anything but infamy? A few scientists, a few men of art and letters. But at the turn of the century a hundred years before that, when Germany was only a name for a culture scattered among petty quarreling states, and there was no material power anywhere in her national organizations, German culture produced Lessing, Herder, Goethe, Schiller, Kant, Hegel, Schopenhauer, Mozart, Beethoven—you can think of many others. The same kind of parallel can be shown in the material confusions and degradations of nineteenth century France when her art and science blazed with glory. On this point, two modern social philosophers, Kroeber and Sorokin, have collected the evidence and the conclusion is inescapable.

This is dwelt on because the fallacy is old, comforting, deepseated and frequently expressed as a rule of history. We can delude ourselves into thinking that for us to turn back from a career of domination, from taking over the world with our gasoline and steel and precarious uranium, would be to forego the great chance to be a great nation and leave a heritage of greatness for the use and admiration of others. Persons and nations are, in moral questions, faced with like decisions. If we look back at the records of the men and women to whom we owe greatness in thought, greatness in artistry, greatness in spirit, we see that almost never were they persons who had power in their own time. Material power and spiritual greatness are almost irrelevant in the lives of men. They are also irrelevant in the history of nations. A man or a country may have either material power or cultural greatness with or without the other. But neither one of them is the cause or the result of the other.

We are in a critical period and we have a choice to make among ideals. Whether or not we are in fact allowed to choose our course may be a debatable question, because we are deep in change and we can neither see clearly, nor control completely, the forces that we ride. We may want to be great in the material sense, dominant, imperialistic, oppressive, and also to do great things with our minds and spirits. But if we seek to gain the city, in the Biblical phrase, we may all too easily lose our own souls, without realizing that it is no better for a nation than it is for a man to want power at too great a cost, or to be unaware of what is paid for it.

We have said that this price is not our freedom at home. There is an evident paradox here. If we can have an empire without giving up our freedom as citizens of our home country, how are we paying for empire by giving up freedom of thought? The examples already given of Rome and Britain, where domestic citizenship got to be more equitable and free during much of the time when the empire was being conquered, ought to indicate an answer. And it seems to me certain that, in Britain in the nineteenth century, the citizen of Birmingham or Aberdeen, busy with his own political and business affairs, did not know what his government was doing in Burma or the Sudan. He believed in the imperial myth and was willing to support it, the myth that his government was bringing benevolent civilization to recalcitrant "niggers" the world over, and when his leaders lied to him as they consistently did, he believed them and was willing, when needed, to die for empire.

If we can choose for our country, if there is still time, what do we want, power in the commonplace imperial sense? Or shall we be a people who want to advance freedom for all peoples, who want to live in the bracing air of freedom of thought at home and be—not the slaves or the beneficiaries of another great empire—but great persons in our own right?

Such a choice, on such a scale as we could make it, has not been made before. If it is possible for us, it will be because we have the institutions, the leaders, and the faiths. And, in fact, I believe that we owe great respect to the national leaders whom we have had in my generation. No one of them, I think, has been a supremely great man in power of mind. They have not been great inventors of values or teachers to the nation. They have been mostly normal and ordinary men, except for courage and political skill. But we cannot find among them anyone who tried consistently to make the American people believe what he thought was a lie. The "golden" lies of Plato's guardians have not ruled us.

We might have had, beginning with Theodore Roosevelt, the kind of leader who would manipulate the sources of public information and the sources of agencies of public opinion, as we saw done in Germany, and as is now being done in many other places. In our country the net of public communication is very wide and very difficult to manage from a central point, but it is also pervasive and influential. A persistent plan to deceive us might have succeeded. If that had been done, it is conceivable that our policies, especially in foreign relations, might have been less vacillating as well as less democratically criticized, and we might have been a mightier power. Having more honest leaders we have been less successfully aggressive than others, and against aggression we have fought back only at the last moment with great cost to ourselves. We have not been the big masterful nation that we sometimes think we ought to be. But if, as a nation, we had been more masterful, our people in this generation would be much less fully aware of what has been going on and would have been less challenged by a painfully real knowledge of the issues. In that case, we might have been a greater nation of lesser persons.

Our question then, "Should a leader deceive the public for the public good?" is not a simple question of good or evil. It is a real choice in political action. Shall we, on the one hand, follow the example of the nations that can set forth uncomplicated simple myths about themselves and their destiny in the world, and believe them, and go on to conquest? Shall we have our own version of the slogan, "Take up the white man's burden"? We, too, can have our imperial adventure, and there are leaders already in training to take us in hand with the right slogans and comforting reassuring myths about our destiny, if we are ready to respond.

But if we want above all things the wisdom and knowledge of free experience, the high privilege of searching for truth by our own powers, we had better give up campaigns against the liberties of others and also—this is harder to do—all campaigns to save other nations from their own errors. We can declare our own faiths and our own gospels, of course, but not with sanctions. Nations that encourage their citizens to be openminded, skeptical, questioning, free, are not good candidates for hegemony. But they have something else. They have a democracy of the spirit and the mind, and what they achieve may really be for the good of others, as well as for themselves.

II

FACT, FICTION, AND REALITY

BY

F. ERNEST JOHNSON

I am disposed to give this address a subtitle: "The Log of a Would-be Truth-Teller." As preacher, writer, researcher, and teacher, I have tried during a fairly long and rather startlingly varied professional life to maintain fidelity to the truth, as I assume all of us at The Institute for Religious and Social Studies have done. But when I attempt now to adapt the well known words of "Invictus," they come out upside down: My head may not be bloody, but it's bowed!

If my early education stressed any one value more than others it was truthfulness. And I have always felt that there was something sound and wholesome in putting truthfulness at the top of the value pyramid, for without mutual trustworthiness human association would never be anything other than some kind of warfare. If we cannot trust our neighbors to tell the truth, there is no enduring reason why we should communicate at all—unless we are bent on deception. And it is interesting to see how broad is the sanction given to truth, even by those who are themselves reckless with it. The most irresponsible propaganda seeks to convict the opposition of untruthfulness. The most accomplished liar will fight back, if he is *called* a liar. So highly is the duty of truthfulness honored in the breach.

Yet in the nature of the case, to make a great virtue out of "telling the truth," involves substantial hazards. It causes all manner of trouble. As for our enemies, if we have such—as we probably should have—their reactions may be discounted. They will get us wrong in any case. But what havoc the mere telling of "the truth, the whole truth, and nothing but the truth" can work with one's friends! Indeed, most of us keep our friends by keeping a good portion of our thoughts about them to ourselves. Utter frankness in very many situations would be sheer boorishness and even cruelty.

The difficulty is that such moral literalism is bound to be abortive. It scatters about so much factual debris as to obscure the most important truth—that we love our friends and really like to have them around. Literal exactness is often an obstacle to reaching the legitimate end of discourse: the faithful rendering of what is essentially in accord with reality. For my part, the upshot of the matter is that I have become convinced that the virtue of truthfulness can be realized only within a framework of equity that transcends considerations that are merely factual. This sometimes includes fiction and myth and it always subordinates everything else to what may be called the ethical realities of an actual situation.

Perhaps it is a vague awareness of this distinction between truthfulness and mere factual exactness that gives rise to the widespread ambivalence with respect to truthfulness that characterizes our culture. There is more than a bit of humor in the anecdote which relates of a certain three presidents of the United States that one could not tell a lie, another could not tell the truth, and a third could not tell the difference! The inhibition against lying we all feel; the great difficulty in adhering strictly to truth is a universal experience; and the tendency to blur the line between them is a well known habit. We honor the man whose "word is as good as his bond." The one unpardonable sin in the financial world, I have been told, is to have "a bad credit." Nobody loves a liar. Yet in a hundred ways we more or less systematically cut the corners in this matter of making the spoken word conform to what we believe to be true. This cannot be due wholly to waywardness. There is confusion as to means and ends.

In many instances urbanity displaces truthfulness. When ladies prefer not to receive a caller, they send word that they are "not at home." Who will not prefer this civil equivocation to the blunt fact: "Madam says she has no desire to look upon your face"? Moreover, the formula is easily rationalized by giving the phrase, "at home," a particular and convenient idiomatic meaning: not receiving callers. Henceforth, visitors are left in comfortable ignorance as to the precise facts of the situation. In some cultures other than ours this kind of procedure is elaborated into a ritual. A friend of mine who was a missionary in China related at his own expense an amusing episode. Eager to avoid committing crude, alien gaucheries, he asked a trusted Chinese friend to tell him frankly about the breaks he was making. But the amiable Oriental assured him that his conduct was unimpeachable; his manners left nothing whatever to be desired. Then he added, apologetically, "I cannot say as much for all your countrymen. Sometimes they do things that offend us. For example . . ." And then followed the damning specifications which, it dawned presently on my friend, were unwitting performances of his own, recited in a way designed to give him a maximum of instruction with a minimum of pain. Who shall say that the Chinese gentleman did not tell more truth about his American friend's *soul* than he told falsehood about his *manners*? And he got across all he wanted to communicate.

What I am leading up to is, of course, an approach to a definition of truth that is different from conventional definitions. I suggest that truth gets its meaning not from correspondence to a preconceived arrangement of the "facts" in the subject matter field, but from what the proposition in question does to the value structure to which it is relevant. A factual narrative leaves the situation as it was. Finding the truth involves restructuring the field of our awareness of the situation. It is reconstructive, often ethically redemptive. Thus the saintly Bishop Bienvenu in Victor Hugo's great novel coolly fabricates a story to save a thief from arrest, and says to him, "Jean Valjean, my brother, you belong no longer to evil, but to good. It is your soul that I am buying for you. I withdraw it from dark thoughts and from the spirit of perdition and I give it to God." The virtue of truth is somehow related to justice and equity. From this viewpoint, facts may actually get in the way of truth.

It is related that a British contemporary of Lloyd George was once asked what sort of man the celebrated Welshman was. "Well," he answered, "I'll tell you. He's the sort of man that won't stand any nonsense from some damn fact." Admittedly that pithy remark is susceptible of more than one interpretation. Yet, it does point to an important aspect of life: that meaning and significance are never found in factual fragments isolated from the context of human experience in which they occur.

It would be an egregious error, however, to suppose that this approach to the problem of truth and truthfulness simplifies the business of ethical living. Quite the contrary. To be sure, escape from bondage to brute fact saves one often from embarrassment. But we noted at the outset that the bias toward exactness in utterance has an authentic quality, in principle. Manipulating facts does put a burden of proof on the manipulator. When violence is done to the letter a strain is put upon the spirit. I once heard a famous woman preacher explaining her views on the merits of "telling the truth" in a situation where the reputation of an indubitably upright person was at stake—where the "literal truth" would do irreparable damage to one who in the distant past had committed a serious fault. Asked pointblank what she would do if required to say yes or no as to the correctness of the accusation she said unequivocally, "I would tell the lie." But when a troubled hearer asked, "Would it not do violence to something within you?" she replied with quick firmness, "Yes! That is the price we pay for living in this world." If truth is understood as bound up with goodness, justice, fairness, the pursuit of truth is no easy matter, but it is endlessly rewarding.

What I am aiming at is strikingly expressed in that widely read little *Story of the Other Wise Man,* by Henry Van Dyke. Confronted by Herod's soldiers in their wild search for the child he had come to adore, at the very entrance of the house where the child was hidden, Artaban declared that the house was empty and gave to the avaricious captain the priceless gift intended for the princely babe. As the captain ordered his men to march on, Artaban turned his face to the East and cried:

"God of truth, forgive my sin! I have said the thing that is not, to save the life of a child. . . . I have spent for man that which was meant for God. Shall I ever be worthy to see the face of the King?"

But from behind him in the shadows came the voice of a woman speaking in tearful joy:

"Because thou hast saved the life of my little one, may the Lord bless thee and keep thee; the Lord make His face to shine upon thee and be gracious unto thee; the Lord lift up His countenance upon thee and give thee peace."

Before going further with the moral and spiritual implications of our topic I would like to point out that what I may call the truth-*versus*-fact dilemma is encountered today in the world of science. In my student days I was much enamored of the study of science, and I supposed that scientific truth—if one had the intelligence and skill to apprehend it—was a clearcut yes-or-no proposition. I supposed the laws of nature were as simple and unequivocal as I then thought the Ten Commandments were! Indeed, science was in those days pretty much a common sense affair. The three dimensional world had not been disturbed by notions of relativity, though among the sophisticated the modern scientific revolution was beginning. How changed the situation is today. Conceptually, science is now quite "out of this world." When matter and energy are thought of as interchangeable, when dimension is conceived as inversely related to velocity, when space is said to be "curved," an entirely new conceptual framework has been introduced. Let me illustrate the point by reference to the theory of light. In their little book, *The Evolution of Physics,* Albert Einstein and Leopold Infeld have an intriguing discussion of the phenomena of light in which this paragraph occurs:

But what is light really? Is it a wave or a shower of photons? Once before we put a similar question when we asked: is light a wave or a shower of light corpuscles? At that time there was every reason for discarding the corpuscular theory of light and accepting the wave theory, which covered all phenomena. Now, however, the problem is much more complicated. There seems no likelihood of forming a consistent description of the phenomena of light by a choice of only one of the two possible languages. It seems as though we must use sometimes the one theory and sometimes the other, while at times we may use either. We are faced with a new kind of difficulty. We have two contradictory pictures of reality;

separately neither of them fully explains the phenomena of light, but together they do! [1]

The obvious, but to the lay mind astonishing, point is that the very effort to be objective and unequivocal in giving an account of physical phenomena, may obscure reality rather than reveal it, for "contradictory pictures of reality" seem to be indispensable. If it is so with the physical world, what may we expect in what philosophers call the axiological world—the world of values?

Let us consider another aspect of the problem which is a matter of every day observation. I refer to the way in which the "truth" is sought in our law courts in civil and criminal cases where the jury trial prevails. In our democratic tradition the right of trial by a jury of one's peers is regarded as a precious heritage. The function of the jury is to determine the facts, and liability or guilt in accord with the facts, within a framework of legal procedure prescribed by the law and the court. Theoretically, the jury system is a great safeguard of liberty. Practically, it has given rise to great concern among jurists, and to cynicism on the part of many observers concerning the capacity of juries to make just and fair decisions. An eminent jurist, Judge Jerome N. Frank of the United States Court of Appeals, has recently made some very disturbing comments about our trials by jury.[2] His discussion goes to the root of one of our commonest democratic assumptions: that trial by jury is a bulwark of freedom—one of the basic human rights in the Western world.

Judge Frank quotes Judge Learned Hand, the late Justice Oliver Wendell Holmes, and the late Chief Justice William Howard Taft, as expressing grave doubts about the merits of jury trials. He remarks that "no sensible business outfit would decide on the competence and honesty of a prospective executive by seeking the judgment of twelve men and women, taken from a group selected almost at random—and from which all those had been weeded out who might have special qualifications for deciding the question."

Yet the historical relation of the institution of trial by jury to the modern democratic movement is well established. Presumably, the

[1] *Evolution of Physics,* New York, Simon & Schuster, 1938, p. 278.
[2] "Something's Wrong with Our Jury System," *Collier's,* December 9, 1950.

Fact, Fiction, and Reality

growth of the system both in England and in America is to be accounted for on the basis of the fear of oppression. Judge Frank thinks the only good argument for trial by jury today is that it provides "escape from decisions by unfit trial judges." But it has come about that democratic governments other than ours have grown cold to jury trials, especially in civil cases, so that trial by jury "cannot be considered an essential part of democratic government."

The paradox presented by this issue is illustrated by citation of an American Bar Association committee's report in 1946. It was argued that jurors must be admonished to "let the law prevail," and to disregard "likes and dislikes"; but the same report contended that "the jury often stands as a bulwark between an individual . . . and an unreasonable law." Judge Frank comments: "Many distinguished lawyers have proclaimed it the glory of the jury system that, thanks to jury-room secrecy, juries can and do defy any law they deem undesirable and, instead, apply secret laws the jurors choose to make."

It thus appears that the very effort to separate the factual from the legal aspects of a case, giving the jury jurisdiction over the one area and the court over the other, has been to a considerable extent abortive. The decisions are likely to be rendered, not on the basis of the facts as evaluated by judicial rule, but in accord with what the jury regards as the requirements of equity. Justice, which in the context of this discussion is a component of the truth we are in quest of, requires a bringing together of factual conclusions and moral judgments. The black-or-white, yes-or-no, either-or quality of factual reporting does not yield equity, and the effort to make it do so may give rise to grievous miscarriages of justice.

It might go without saying that I am not here trying to dispose, off hand, of an important and complex judicial question. My purpose is rather to illustrate by reference to one of our best established institutions, the complexity of the quest for truth in human relationships. It is strange how complacently we face contradictory situations without seeking their inner meaning.

Let us look at the problem from another angle. In my early professional life I attempted to be something of a social reformer. I was caught up in a zealous crusade for law enforcement in a community where the authorities were lax. It seemed simple enough, even though dogged persistence was required. Surely a man was either a law abiding citizen or he was not. If he was selling liquor without a license or violating the Sunday closing laws, what more did one need to know? Present the evidence and let the law take its course. But I was to learn that it was not so simple. The law might take its course—and it might not. But the important point is that merely establishing the fact that a law had been violated, told us nothing very significant about a man's character as a whole, about what he really thought about his own behavior, or about the attitude toward him of the community of which he was a part.

When studying the Prohibition situation in the 1920's, I was somewhat startled to find that highly respected citizens, eminent jurists among them, were ready to pronounce the Prohibition law morally wrong, quite without reference to any sociological data that might support it, just as eminent churchmen insisted that the law was indubitably right, no matter how great a body of facts might be cited as discrediting the Prohibition regime. Facts acquire their meaning from a context in which value attitudes have preponderance. This is why during the Prohibition era we witnessed the anomaly of eminent jurists and other outstanding citizens regarding with complacency the nullification of a federal law which had been upheld by the Supreme Court. Rightly or wrongly, they thought the demands of equity and order justified the infraction of a particular statute. In *fact* their attitude was criminal. In truth and equity, as they saw the situation, they were reformers.

A friend of mine who is a professional economist once commented facetiously on the findings of another economist in a study of social waste. The latter had decided arbitrarily to call all beverage liquor "waste" if the alcoholic content exceeded ten per cent. "Why," said his critic, "I know a lot of people who call any drink 'waste' that is *less* than ten per cent alcohol!" So it is with all judgments involving facts, when the facts are related to value judgments. On the basis of the same factual account one person finds true what another finds false. The essence of bad propaganda, which today grievously threatens the democratic process, is the setting of facts in a chosen frame-

Fact, Fiction, and Reality 33

work of desires and prejudices which has anti-social implications. I often feel impatient with social idealists—some of them cultural anthropologists—who suppose that by merely *proving* racial equality as a fact, they are going to induce prejudiced people to treat all men as their equals. So long as deep antipathies endure, people have no difficulty in making facts fit into their prejudices. The truth about race relations is not a set of anthropological facts but a spiritual experience, to be validated empirically by those who have the courage to enter into it.

This is not to say that facts are unimportant, but that their importance has to be contextually appraised. Nor is it to say, as many people have said, that there is no such thing as objectivity in *reporting* facts. It is the business of an investigator to be objective in reporting facts, and to all intents this is quite possible for one who has intelligence, training, and a good conscience. But facts as assimilated by the public—any public—are never neutral: they are colored by human desires and intentions. Brute facts in the hands of rascals readily become weapons of mass destruction.

Another aspect of our problem is the relation between facts and the purposeful fictions by which ideals are given substance in the refinement of human experience. We are wont, for example, to speak of traits such as honesty, unselfishness, and justice, as if they were actually realized in experience. We say, "He is an honest man; he is a just man." Everyone knows these are fictions, for no one is wholly honest or wholly just, if absolute standards are applied. Yet we need objectification of our ideals. We must be able to see them personified, in order that they may be dynamic. In a broad context of human judgment and aspiration it is "truer" to call Abraham Lincoln "Honest Abe," than to hedge about the appellation with the qualifications that factual accuracy might require—qualifications that Lincoln himself would have been the first to stipulate.

All our general affirmations in the field of ethics have a certain eulogistic quality in their reference to human nature. Take, for example, the affirmation that all men are created equal. Nothing is more patently untrue, if factual accuracy is the standard of judgment. It derives its validity from what we feel to be an authentic imperative to *treat all men as equals*. T. V. Smith has suggested that we should regard equality as "an ethical and political fiction, just as in law the treating of a corporation as a person is called a legal fiction." The word, "fiction," here signifies that "certain aspects of the case are consciously overlooked out of practical motivation." However, "since it does certain violence to our knowledge as a whole, we confess that injustice by admitting it a fiction, but one practically justified. By its fruits rather than by its roots we judge it."[3]

It is but a step from this conception to the use of myth (*mythos*) in theology. To many people the characterization of the creation story and the story of "the fall" in Genesis as mythological, is a shocking relegation of them to the category of prescientific myths. While the use of the term, "myth," in connection with articles of faith, is no doubt arguable, it misses the point completely to identify the ideas thus denoted with the naive notions of primitive men. When a mythological conception embodied in a theological doctrine has mediated religious experience to generation after generation of believers, it should be patent that something elemental and authentic is involved. The doctrine affirms a quality of life, an aspect of reality, which can be more vividly and more arrestingly expressed in the form of historical narrative than in any other way. Who shall say that this is less valid than the affirmation that all men are created equal, which a verbal literalism would inevitably reject as absurd?

What, after all, is a creed? Undoubtedly, in their original use, the creeds of Christendom were devices for the preservation of strict orthodoxy—for excluding what were regarded as dangerous heresies. On no other basis would the exhaustive and repetitive explicitness of some of the ancient creeds be intelligible. Even so, it is interesting to note that the Apostles' Creed was early known as the "Old Roman Symbol," and that the theological discipline embracing the study of the creeds was traditionally known as "symbolics." The point I wish to make, however, is that the historic creeds function as something quite other than statements of fact. A creed can no more be defined

---

[3] *The American Philosophy of Equality*, Chicago, The University of Chicago Press, 1927, pp. 268, 269.

as a series of factual propositions than a flag can be defined as a series of strips of dyed muslin.

William P. Montague has discussed in very suggestive fashion the problem arising from imputing factual validity to religious creeds. "The heart," he writes, "craves a set of absolute certainties which the mind, however slightly touched with the mood and spirit of rational inquiry, cannot but reject or question." Religious myths, he holds, have a quality that makes them irreplaceable. "To demand that they be reduced to the level of scientific theories and defended or refuted, is worse than false: it is irrelevant to their real significance and value, which . . . consists in the moral ideals which they incarnate in the life of the soul." The rival claims of the intellect and the spirit present a dilemma. "I suggest," says Professor Montague, "that we can master this dilemma only by holding fast to both of its horns. Let us retain the creed of our cultural past and use our own present creed not as a substitute for the other but as a supplement to it. . . . The one creed will be *sung,* the other will be *said*. Or if we do not literally sing the ancient creed, the mood and temper of its utterance should be that of song. The time-honored symbols will deeply move our hearts by expressing the sentiments and ideals of our fathers." But there is needed also "a sterner and colder confession of what at a given time the members of a given Church believe on grounds of reason to be objectively and existentially true." [4]

There will be different opinions about any proposals for resolving the tension between the claims of the mind for factual exactness and the claims of the spirit for energizing symbols which embody unequivocal affirmations of faith. But surely a workable reconciliation of these claims is one of our major needs.

I am reminded of some memorable words spoken by one of my great teachers in philosophy, the late Professor Woodbridge. In one of those characteristic moments when he combined profound insight with quaint humor he exclaimed, "Who is right about the moon —the astronomer, who describes her cold, barren, dreary surface, or

---

[4] *Liberal Theology,* David E. Roberts and Henry Pitney Van Dusen, editors, New York, Charles Scribner's Sons, 1942, pp. 155, 158, 159.

the poet who apostrophizes her: 'O Thou Queen of the Night'!" Who indeed?

I have given a very sketchy analysis of a difficult problem. In a sense it is a problem of communication, and in that sense it is basically psychological. But essentially it is a philosophical and moral problem, for it concerns the communication of what is, so to say, ultimately real, and as such necessarily overflows the walls of every vehicle of communication. The question has been implicit throughout the discussion: How can discourse be justified which disregards "the facts"? The answer, it seems to me, is that imaginative devices in communication are justified when, though they take liberties with the cold facts, they are effectual means of conveying vital truth.

III

ON THE JUSTIFIABLE GROUNDS OF DISOBEDIENCE TO LAW

BY

ROGER N. BALDWIN

A long experience in defending civil liberties for those, among others, who asserted their moral or constitutional rights above some law, inclines me to a not unnatural partisanship for moral lawbreaking. It may be suggested also that my own record reinforces that partisanship, as I was one of those who in the First World War chose jail rather than yield my conscience to a soldier's role. There were then no other choices. But I am sufficiently detached in time, if not conviction, from that experience to deal quite impersonally with the lessons of my professional contacts as a defender of assorted under dogs—and occasionally some of the upper.

The very essence of civil liberties, it will be agreed, is the maintenance of freedom of thought and of conscience against all restraints, whether by law or by private force. Although the American Civil Liberties Union, which I have long represented, of course accepts as ultimate law the decisions of the United States Supreme Court, it does not thereby cease trying to change them where they appear not to square with the principles of civil liberty. And not without hope, for the Supreme Court has not been above reversing a former majority. Despite the Court's opinions, the Union has even continued to aid those who violate valid laws, but only where resistance rests on loyalty to higher moral authority than the state. For it will be conceded without argument that concepts of liberty are not to be measured by whatever courts may declare lawful at the moment.

Progress is manifestly on the side of the pioneers of moral lawbreaking, for it is through the rebels and heretics of their times that most political, religious, and social advances have been won. Traitors always fail, for if they succeed they become patriots. Political progress owes a great debt to successful traitors. The thousands who, sustained by conscience, resisted the Inquisition and went to their tortured deaths, assured the secular state and freedom of religious dissent. The abolitionists who held the fugitive slave law good only for breaking, and the Thoreaus who justified the high "Duty of Civil Disobedience," paved the road to the emancipation. The Gandhis who in all lands subjugated by imperialist powers flouted the conqueror's law by non-violent resistance, and even those who resorted to conventional force, were acclaimed as liberators of oppressed peoples entitled to their national independence. Lawbreakers and benefactors all!

These historic examples on the grand scale are matched by scores in our own history on the smaller. In a country founded largely by dissenters fleeing Old World tyrannies, we have from the beginning recognized the moral basis of disobedience to unjust laws. Early New England colonial history is replete with their resistance. So great was the revolutionary spirit of unlawful resistance to lawful tyranny, that Jefferson was moved to observe that the tree of liberty not only is nourished by the blood of martyrs but can be preserved only by occasional revolution—about once every twenty years, he figured.

In our own day we have seen a many sided conflict between law and a higher morality. We have, I may add, also seen one between law and a lowly self-serving morality—in the wholesale lawbreaking of the Prohibition years. But the higher morality is evident among other conflicts in the claims of conscientious objection to war service on religious and humanitarian grounds, in the refusal on religious grounds to salute the flag, in the opposition of conscientious teachers and public employees to taking special oaths of loyalty, in refusals to comply with the laws of racial segregation, and in defiance of bans on peaceful assemblage or picketing.

In most of these conflicts, and in others of like character, the moral claims, dramatized by lawbreaking, have resulted in ultimate vindication in law. Most of the Supreme Court cases involving civil rights start with a lawbreaker challenging the constitutionality of a law, an order, a denial of somebody's right. Without the moral lawbreaker, taking his chances of jail or vindication, the principles could not have been tested. Liberty, observed a well known political scientist, depends in the last analysis on that "anarchist residuum" in every society composed of those rebels willing to assert higher social welfare against law. Whether they do so for the general good or for the interests of a particular section of society with a claim to the higher loyalty, makes no difference in the effect. Labor's fight for its rights, for instance, becomes society's gain.

Of the many minorities asserting such claims with which I have had a considerable experience, two of little general repute stand out as contributing greatly to the advance of American law and practice of civil rights—the Industrial Workers of the World—that militant organization of largely migratory workers which aroused such fear in the first quarter of the century by its non-violent direct methods of challenging restrictive laws—and Jehovah's Witnesses, a worldwide association of Fundamentalist Christians who proclaim the glad tidings of salvation by tract distributing, phonograph playing and word of mouth.

Both organizations, though so diverse, had much in common as minorities. Both were bitterly fought by public authorities all over the country, by denying rights of peaceful meeting in public places and of distributing literature. Both were charged with seeking the overthrow of society, disloyalty, and disturbance of the peace. The unspoken charge was quite different: they disturbed the peace of mind of powerful interests. They were rebels—one to the economic system, the other to patriotism. They did not conform to accepted obligations of good citizens. They did not vote or serve on juries. They refused military service. If they were not violent, they at least made their opponents violent, and hence were a menace to law and order.

By persistence and organized courage the Industrial Workers had not only won by 1917 the rights of free speech and assembly in scores of cities where they had been denied, but had improved wages and hours. The organization died out after the First World War, as a result of internal dissensions, government war prosecutions, and changes in industry which reduced the role of migratory workers. But its contribution to American civil liberties remained, as a testimonial to an amazing record of solidarity and determination in asserting what the members regarded as their rights as workers—"industrial citizens." They had an articulate philosophy of higher law than that of sheriffs, police, and city councils, and they practiced it. And they won largely by direct action, not by appeal to the courts. Their direct action consisted in flooding with soapbox speakers any town where free speech had been denied, thus clogging the courts and filling the jails so full that no more could be arrested. They would then be turned loose—to speak and organize. The moral law had triumphed out of inability to enforce the written; and out of some sense of guilt, no doubt, over making free speech a crime.

Jehovah's Witnesses, who did not come into wide public notice until recent years—though they existed long as "Russellites" (named from their founder, Pastor Russell) and later as the International Bible Students Association—based their claims to freedom from restraint on precisely the same principles as the I.W.W. They held that they had a moral and constitutional right to campaign for the Lord in their own peaceful way, distributing literature in public places or from door to door, ringing doorbells, playing phonograph records of their propaganda, carrying placards in the streets, and refusing to salute the flag or permitting their children to do so in the public schools. They exercised merely the inherent constitutional right to be a nuisance.

Blocked all over the country by restrictions, often made to order to combat them, they did what the I.W.W. did not do—they resorted to the courts for vindication of their claims not only to constitutional rights of free speech, press and assembly, but to freedom of religion to engage in any practice not harmful to society. For ten long years they carried to the Supreme Court of the United States case after case they had lost in the lower. Probably no single organization in American history has more often appealed to the Supreme Court for vindication of civil rights, nor more often succeeded. Not a single major issue was lost. And what was established in a whole series of

On the Justifiable Grounds of Disobedience to Law 41

decisions not only assured freedom of religion in new interpretations for Jehovah's Witnesses, but for all American citizens an extension of their civil rights.

As direct results of the restraints contested by Jehovah's Witnesses, no state or city may today license or tax the distribution of literature in public places. Nor may any state or city prohibit or license the door to door distribution of literature. No discrimination may be practiced by public officials in permitting the use of loud speakers in public places—but they may, presumably and rightly, be totally banned as public nuisances. No school board may require children to salute the flag as a condition of attending public school.

The Witnesses lost three minor legal rounds among their many contentions—one, their part time evangelists may not be classified as ministers within the meaning of the draft law; second, children may not engage in distribution of their literature, in violation of child labor laws; and third, literature distribution may be barred on private "company" property. Of these three losses, only the first seriously affected the claimed liberties of the Witnesses, for thousands of their young men chose to go to prison in World War II, rather than to accept any service after being denied exemptions as ministers. Of all conscientious objectors imprisoned, they made up the overwhelming number.

Almost all this protracted litigation to establish constitutional rights was the result of what the Witnesses regarded, and not without reason, as persecution. Everywhere they have resisted it, abroad as in the United States. Hundreds, if not thousands, of their members have suffered imprisonment and even death in other lands for refusing to obey "manmade" law. Their attitude is one of unyielding obedience to what they conceive to be the commands of Jehovah, as interpreted by their leaders. They have not sought martyrdom, but they accept it as the price of unyielding faith. Their otherworldliness prompts them to ignore the obligations of citizenship, but their lack of national patriotism does not in their view deny them the rights of citizenship. The courts have, on the whole, justified their refusal to obey restrictive laws. Where they have still refused after the Supreme Court denied their claims—as with draft exemption for their agents as ministers—they rest their disobedience not on constitutional grounds, which they could no longer argue, but on moral grounds. No reasonable man can deny the right to resist a law in conflict with conscience and to take the consequences in jail. And it will not be denied that a lot of historic advances for liberty have been made in jails.

No such defiance of law by an annoying minority wins public approval, and Jehovah's Witnesses, like heretics before them, have faced an unsympathetic and often hostile majority. Even among religious communions they have not had a sympathetic hearing, though the rights they fought for square with the principles to which almost all religions pay tribute. But the Witnesses are hostile themselves to "organized religion," particularly Catholicism, as "rackets." They sought no allies, and they had none. Their lone struggle won little appreciation of their service to the far wider cause than their own; not even the thousands of their young men who endured uncomplainingly long years in prison for conscience aroused nearly the sympathetic interest as did the comparatively few objectors from other religious communions. The Witnesses were "queer" and aloof. Yet it is just such stout resistance as theirs which tests the basic strength of democratic liberties.

The Witnesses are but one, though a telling, example of the conflicts that arise in a democratic society between demands of the state and religious liberties or conscience. Accommodation between them has been the usual outcome in our country, with the claims of a loyalty above the state generally recognized where they involve no damage to society. A line of course is drawn at anti-social practices. Polygamy may not be sanctioned in the name of religion, nor ceremonies characterized by the use of rattlesnakes as divine messengers (except among the Indians who know how to handle them)! But a flag need not be saluted contrary to the command of the Lord, as the Witnesses have it, nor a man compelled to bear arms against his religious belief.

A fair general conclusion on the ground of social ethics is that citizens are justified in disobeying law when it conflicts with a higher religious loyalty, or with a social conscience, as in the struggle against slavery or racial segregation; or when law appears to violate constitutional rights or those natural rights, so-called, which men instinctively and universally assert—freedom of expression and association. And the case might fairly be stretched to breaking law to save the lives of others, or even to taking the life of another in those mercy-killings in which juries have so often freed the killer. These, too, are higher social loyalties than the law.

Respect for law, I agree, is basic to democracy, or our society would not hang together in reasonable peace. But disrespect for tyrannical laws, not made by popular consent, or for laws violative of basic human rights, made like the fugitive slave act by a divided nation, is a social virtue. Law not resting on popular assent is worth little anyhow in practice. It is either ignored or nullified, like Prohibition, and like the wide range of unenforceable taboos on irregular sexual conduct exposed by Dr. Kinsey as commonplaces of American private life.

But where law even with popular assent denies to a minority the liberties it demands in the name of God or the social good, a critical conflict arises on whose solution depends the test of democracy. For democracy's ultimate sanction lies in its free play of personal and group creative powers; and it is not for law in the name of the majority to determine what minority is creative and useful and what not. Democracy knows no orthodoxy. The flow of progress lies in enduring dissent, heresy, criticism, and challenge to accepted institutions. The highway for the prophets of the future can be assured only as it is open on equal terms to the guardians of the past. Whether Jehovah's Witnesses, whose example I have stressed, are regarded as the vanguard of the hosts at Armageddon or the relics of an ancient fundamentalism, is irrelevant. Their sacrificial testimony to faith in the inherent claims of the human spirit above law has not only practically served the advancement of our democracy, but points up a universal lesson in the nature of growth toward a free society.

IV

ON THE LIMITS OF JUSTIFIABLE DISOBEDIENCE

BY

FRANZ L. NEUMANN

When I started my work on this paper, I thought the answer to the question would be easy. One could, so I believed, easily state the conditions under which the citizen may refuse obedience to positive law. The more I thought and the deeper I went into literature, the less became my certainty. To be sure, I could easily present a formula —I could refer to natural law, to inalienable rights—but a formula has a meaning only if and when it is applied to concrete circumstances, and is quite empty when it is abstractly stated. I am afraid, therefore, that my answer will be quite unsatisfactory. I shall be far more concerned with pointing out the difficulties inherent in the affirmative and in the negative, than in a formulation of a theory of my own.

The problem is, of course, quite old. In its extreme form, it involves the right to kill a tyrant. As it is my general conception that problems of political philosophy are best understood if the marginal cases are clearly stated, I shall begin with the extreme manifestation of the right of resistance: the so-called regicide or tyrannicide problem.

I

1. The history of regicide begins with an historical error. In the ancient tradition,[1] the assassination of Hipparchus (the son of Pisis-

[1] Cf. especially Hans Georg Schmidt, *Die Lehre vom Tyrannenmord*, Tuebingen, 1901.

tratus) by Harmodius and Aristogiton (514 B.C.E.) was hailed as the first example of the removal of a tyrant by freedom loving conspirators. Yet we know that the murder was entirely motivated by a personal grudge against the tyrant and not directly by political considerations. Still, it is this assassination which gave rise to the powerful tradition which continued up to the seventeenth century (the rise of secular absolutism) and which received a new impetus with the ascendance of totalitarianism. If one analyzes the reaction of public opinion to the attempt on Hitler's life (July 20, 1944) one is struck by the fact that the right to assassinate him was never questioned by the Western world, which merely complained of the lack of its success.

If I am right in this, the question posed is, indeed, quite vital. Perhaps, through this analysis, the general problem of the right of resistance may receive some clarification.

2. To the ancients, a problem apparently did not exist. One ought to expect that Plato would discuss the tyrannicide problem. But he does not. Yet the first genuine assassination of a tyrant for political reasons was carried out by two of his students. In 353, Clearchus, tyrant of Pontic Heraclea was killed for patriotic reasons by Chion and Leonidas. Plato, and there is virtually no disagreement on this point, assumes that a tyrant forfeits his life. Books 8 and 9 of his *Republic* show this quite clearly. The same is true of Aristotle. He introduces a distinction between two types of tyranny: the tyrant *absque titulo* (the usurper); and the tyrant *quoad exercitio* (the legitimate ruler who violates the law). But a philosophical analysis of the conditions under which the one or the other may be removed is not to be found in Aristotle's work.

3. Yet, it is impossible to ape today the, let us say, attitude of nonchalance of the ancients toward tyrannicide. It is quite closely tied up with their general philosophical theory that man exists only as a citizen of the *polis*. If man's existence is solely, or primarily, a political one, then tyrannicide follows: the life of the ruler is then dependent upon his usefulness for the city. This philosophy we cannot accept. To us, man exists quite independently of the political organization in which he lives.

On the Limits of Justifiable Disobedience

Consequently, St. Augustine [2] answered the tyrannicide problem quite differently. God, so he says, gave the Romans Augustus, as well as Nero, Constantine, as well as Julian the Apostate. In rejecting the right to suicide, St. Augustine reiterates that nobody may arbitrarily kill a man, not even a condemned criminal. Two exceptions merely are admitted: authorization by a just law; and a special command by God [3] St. Augustine is, however, fully aware of the dangers inherent in the two exceptions. To ward off too wide an interpretation of the exceptions, he even criticizes the Old Testament generally preferring the New Testament, and even doubts that Moses was right in killing the Egyptian.[4]

4. This Augustinian position, however, did not prevail for long. While I cannot cite here the long history of regicide doctrines, the emphatic affirmation of regicide in John of Salisbury's *Policraticus*, the reluctant and hedged in acceptance by St. Thomas Aquinas, make it important to realize that all protagonists of tyrannicide draw their illustrations from the Old Testament and from antiquity, and discard the Augustinian position. It is this conflict between the two Christian traditions which shook the Christian world in the early fifteenth century. On November 23, 1407, Duke Louis of Orléans was assassinated by two noblemen on the instigation of Duke John of Burgundy.[5] For more than ten years did the "Justification of the Duke of Burgundy," by Jean Petit, excite the world: [6] Everybody may kill a tyrant, oaths become invalid, and immoral means are justified against a tyrant—thus can his statements be summarized. The Council of Paris (1413–1414) dealt exclusively with this issue and at it Jean de Gerson, chancellor of the University of Paris, undertook to restore the Augustinian position. Yet the majority of the theologians did not follow him, although Gerson formally obtained

---

[2] Cf. Max Lossen, *Die Lehre vom Tyrannenmord in der Christlichen Zeit*, Muenchen, 1894. All quotations from St. Augustine are from Lossen's paper.
[3] *De civitate Dei*, Book I, Ch. 17 and 21; Book V, Ch. 19 and 21.
[4] *Op. cit.*, Book I, Ch. 26; and cf. *Faustum*, Book 22, Ch. 70 in *Migne*, 42, 444.
[5] On this see Friedrich Schoenstedt, *Der Tyrannenmord im Spaetmittelalter*, Berlin, 1938.
[6] A. Coville, *Jean Petit, la question du tyrannicide au commencement du XV e siècle*, Paris, 1932.

a victory. The Council of Constance reaffirmed, at least in the decisive parts, the tyrannicide justification of Jean Petit. There exist, of course, fundamental differences between the ancient and the medieval justification of tyrannicide. While the former found the legitimacy in the good of the *polis,* the latter found it in natural law and in the feudal relationship between lord and vassal. Whether any of these are adequate, shall concern us later.

5. While political murder was, of course, widely practiced in the Renaissance period, theories about tyrannicide, are absent. One is more concerned with its psychology and sociology, that is, with the technological aspects of political murder, than with its morality. Consequently, we call these doctrines of politics *arcana* doctrines, because they debate exclusively the means by which a political end can be most rationally achieved.

6. The new wave of doctrinal discussions concerning the right of resistance and the right to kill a tyrant follows the Reformation. We know that neither Luther nor Calvin advocated revolt against the authority of the prince and that both rejected tyrannicide. Yet, while Luther's attitude is fairly unambiguous, Calvin's is by no means so. While the histories of political thought usually stress that Calvin permitted resistance by those organs of the state which are constitutionally entrusted with restraints of monarchical power (such as Estates), one usually overlooks the farreaching statement at the very end of his *Institutes:* [7] "In two ways God restrains the fury of tyrants: either by raising up from among their own subjects open avengers who rid the people of their tyranny, or by employing for that purpose the rage of man whose thoughts and contrivances are totally different, thus overturning one tyranny by means of another." While the first half of the statement envisages the Cromwellian type of a select secular savior, the second half is probably not more than a sociological analysis of the phenomenon that a tyranny may breed a countertyranny. Thus, his statement may perhaps not be conceived as a justification of tyrannicide.

Yet, whatever may have been the attitudes of the reformers them-

[7] Book IV, Ch. XX, 31, I quote the more precise Aphorism No. 99 in the translation of Henry Beveridge.

selves, those of their followers exhibit the whole range of attitudes: absolute submission to secular power; via passive obedience; to active resistance and regicide. In the Protestant Monarchomachs, the right to resist is unquestioned: John Poynet, Christopher Goodman in England, Jean de Poltrot, François Hotman, Junius Brutus in France, to mention but a few. The theory of resistance is Calvinism—or as it was understood by this political party.

7. A new theory of resistance was, however, developed by the Catholic party, particularly by the French Jean Boucher [8] and the Spaniard Juan de Mariana.[9] This theory is allegedly democratic. God invested the people with political power; they may, in a case of tyranny, revoke the agreement with the ruler, depose, and even kill him.

II

Let us leave the historical survey here. It cannot but make us despair, if we hope, through a mere historical analysis, to arrive at a conclusion whether or not, and under what conditions, a right of resistance is permissible. What history shows is merely that all political doctrines were used for purely political purposes: resistance was justified when it suited the interests of a group and was rejected when it did not.

1. In all the theories which I have sketched, one simple problem cannot be answered: who makes the decision whether and when a right to resist exists.

In the case of the ancients: who decides what the good of the *polis* requires; for the medieval theories, it is either the Church or the secular powers which claim the authority to make the decision; in the monarchomachic struggles, the religious party decides; in the so-called democratic theories—the people.

We may give to these various theories of resistance three names: We may call the ancient theory a *functional* theory—resistance is

---

[8] *Sermons de la simulée conversion et nullité de la prétendue absolution de Henri de Bourbon*, Paris, 1594.
[9] *De Rege et Regis Institutione* (transl. by G. A. Moore as *The King and the Education of the King*), Washington, D.C., 1948.

justified, if and where the ruler no longer fulfils his proper function.

We may call the medieval, *natural law* theories—resistance is justified, if and where the ruler forgets the restraints imposed upon him by natural law, or does not rule according to these precepts.

We may call the modern, *democratic* theories of resistance, for obvious reasons.

To decide upon the validity of the three theories, we must attempt a more theoretical analysis.

2. Here, the question hinges upon an analysis of the meaning of the term, "right." This term may mean first: the power to act by grant of positive law; second, the power to act by grant of an objective natural law; third, the power to act is deemed to be inherent in the very nature of man (what may be called a natural right).

3. Is it really significant to interpret the term, "right," as a term of positive law? Two possibilities exist. Positive law may expressly or implicitly prohibit resistance. In that case, no problem of positive law exists.

Or, positive law may expressly or implicitly permit the right of resistance. In our Declaration of Independence, the first part of the second paragraph establishes under certain conditions "the right of the people to alter or abolish (any form of government), and to institute new government." Yet the Declaration does not contribute to our problem. It is the "people" [10] alone who can lawfully make a revolution, the individual right of resistance is not encompassed by it.

4. Let us take a modern case: the Constitution of the State of Hessen in Western Germany. Article 147 provides: "It is the right and duty of everyman to resist unconstitutionally exercised public power." Surely a well intentioned provision inserted after a speech by the then Communist deputy Bauer (now purged by the Soviets) who insisted on everyman's right and duty to defend the Constitution against all anti-democratic movements.[11] But has it any meaning? The answer is, no. And this negative answer must be given to

---

[10] See on this Carl L. Becker, *The Declaration of Independence*, New York, 1942, p. 9.

[11] This constitutional provision is discussed by Carl Heyland in his book, *Das Widerstandsrecht des Volkes*, Tuebingen, 1950, p. 85.

all who expect a solution of the problem from positive law, even if the concrete provisions of positive law go beyond the formulation of the Hessian constitution. Let us assume a constitution provides that everyone may lawfully resist any infringement of the state with one's inalienable right of life and liberty. This provision becomes meaningful, only if there is an ultimate organ (such as an independent judiciary) deciding whether or not the state did unjustly interfere with my rights, or, in the case of Hessen, the constitutional court will ultimately decide whether public power was unconstitutionally exercised. One may say that this is perfectly adequate. For practical purposes it may be more often than not. But sometimes, it is not. Certainly those who did entrust their rights to the judiciary of the Weimar Republic could not hope to have their rights preserved. The German judiciary was then a political organ of the anti-democratic counter-revolution and not an independent judiciary for the protection of civil rights. Whether this is radically different today is difficult to say. But even in our judicial system, although it is infinitely superior to the German, we may encounter politically biased judges and juries which express mob sentiments rather than a considered judgment of rationally thinking people.

So that, even for practical purposes, the positive enactment of the right of resistance does not always help. That it is not satisfactory from a theoretical point of view, is obvious, because the decision does not rest with the individual but with some governmental organ.

5. Do the doctrines of natural law provide an adequate theoretical base? That is: can the term, "right," be interpreted to mean either a power flowing from an objective system of natural law or deemed to be inherent in the very nature of man? If we mean by natural law the Thomistic system, the answer is simple, only if we accept with it the authority of the Catholic Church to decide if and when secular powers have violated the objective norms of natural law. If we do not, that is, if we accept the normative system without its institutionalization, then we face the problem which Kant faced in his political philosophy. He started with the doctrine of natural right and ended with the postulate of absolute submission to the political powers that are. "Freedom," so he says, "is the independence of the compulsory

will of another, and in so far as it can co-exist with the freedom of all according to a universal law, it is the one sole, original, inborn right, belonging to every man by virtue of his humanity." [12] Yet the decision whether my freedom can co-exist with that of others lies solely with the sovereign state. Why? Because the right of resistance is incompatible with the notion of the state. I quote: "For whoever would restrict the supreme power of the State must have more, or, at least, equal power, as compared with the power that is to be restricted; and if competent to command the subjects to resist, such a one would also have to be able to protect them, and if he is to be considered capable of judging what is right in every case he may also publicly order resistance. But such a one, and not the actual authority, would then be the supreme power; which is contradictory." [13] This argument is logically unassailable. It merely expresses the theoretical difficulty in which modern political theory finds itself.

6. The problem of political philosophy, and its dilemma, is the reconciliation of freedom and coercion. With the emergence of the money economy, we encounter the modern state as an institution which claims the monopoly of coercive power, in order to provide a secure basis upon which trade and commerce may flourish and the citizens may enjoy the benefits of their labor. But by creating this institution, by acknowledging its sovereign power, the citizen created an instrument that could and frequently did deprive him of protection and of the boon of his work. Consequently, while justifying the sovereign power of the state, he sought at the same time to justify limits upon the coercive power. The history of modern political thought is the history of this attempt to justify might and right, law and power. There is no political theory which does not do both things. The most absolutive theories (Hobbes and Spinoza) which, at first sight, reject individual right, admit them, however, through a back door: Hobbes by transforming the sovereign into a kind of business aspect of society with all the power he wants if he conducts his business well, but with none if he fails to secure order and security; Spinoza by his formula that right equals might, permits any social

[12] *Metaphysik der Sitten, Rechtslehre* (Einleitung B), transl. Hastie, p. 56.
[13] *Ibid.*, Part II, Section 1 (Allgemeine Anmerkung A), p. 175.

On the Limits of Justifiable Disobedience

group that is powerful enough to transform its social power into right, to change from an *alterius iuris* into a *sui iuris*. Locke, the protagonist of right and law, felt compelled to admit the prerogative power authorizing the monarch to act without law, and sometimes even against it, if and when right and law tend to jeopardize the state.[14] Put in a short formula: freedom is not only liberty against government, but equally liberty through government. The two aspects may harmonize in some historical situations; they may not in others. They may harmonize for some groups in society and not for others.

7. Can we accept the Kantian solution of the conflict? This solution is merely the reformulation of Rousseau's idea of the general will as the great harmonizer of the collective interest of the nation with the interests of its citizens. Yet the democratic theory provides no solution to the right of resistance. A genetic theory (the theory of the origin of political power) does not, thereby, make the exercise of power legitimate. The democratic majority may violate rights. A wrong cannot possibly become right because the majority wills it so. Perhaps it, thereby, becomes a greater wrong.

But it is argued that the right of resistance while germane to all non-democratic political systems, is really expendable in a democracy, because the democratic system provides ample relief for minority views. The very system of democracy is thus conceived to be a kind of institutionalized right of resistance. This argument, however, is fallacious. There is, already, a pragmatic objection to this view. Whether or not a democracy really protects minority views, is open to judgment. Different views may be held in regard to each and every one of the various types of democracy. Consequently, for those who allege, rightly or wrongly, that the system does not adequately safeguard their rights, the individual right of resistance still remains a problem. One cannot, theoretically, answer this view by referring to the independent judiciary—for reasons already discussed.

Consequently, while democracy certainly eases the problem of the individual's right of resistance, it does not eliminate it.

---

[14] The foregoing is taken from my Introduction to *Montesquieu, the Spirit of the Laws*, Hafner Library, New York, 1949, pp. 23, 32.

8. We are thus thrown back to the doctrine of natural rights (or natural law). Here, a distinction is vital, that, namely, between the theoretical base of the natural rights doctrine and its concrete manifestations.

The latter (namely, a natural law system with concrete inhibitions and norms) is theoretically untenable. The criticisms of Hume [15] and Hegel [16] are unanswerable.[17] All these systems are philosophically arbitrary. They endow man, in his state of nature, with certain qualities and then deduce a concrete system of natural rights (and duties) from the arbitrary statement of the nature of man. Both Hume and Hegel (and many others, particularly Georges Sorel) [18] make the obvious point: that the opposite view is always conceivable. As Hegel puts it,[19] the "guiding principle of the *a priori* is the *a posteriori.*" Similarly, Rousseau formulated his objection to the natural law doctrines: "He (namely, the natural law theorist) begins by casting about for rules which, in their own interest, it would be well for man to agree upon; and then, without any further proof than the supposed advantage thus resulting, he proceeds to dignify this body of rules by the name of Natural Law. All the philosophers of his school have followed the same method. The result is that all the definitions of these learned men, in standing contradiction with each other, agree in this conclusion only: that it is impossible to understand, impossible, therefore, to obey, the law of nature without being a deep reasoner and a very great metaphysician. And that is only another way of saying that, for the establishment of society, man must have made use of the wisdom which is, in fact, only gradually acquired by a small minority of men and that with the utmost difficulty, in the bosom of society itself." [20]

---

[15] On Hume's criticism (in his *Treatise of Human Nature*) see particularly George H. Sabine, *A History of Political Theory*, New York, 1937, pp. 598–616.
[16] In *Ueber die Wissenschaftlichen Behandlungsarten des Naturrechts*, 1802.
[17] On the whole problem see my "Types of Natural Law," in *Studies in Philosophy and Social Science*, VIII, 1939, pp. 338–361. I do not, however, fully maintain this position.
[18] In *Le Procès de Socrate*, Paris, 1889.
[19] *Op. cit., Schriften zur Politik und Rechtsphilosophie*, Leipzig, 1913, p. 339.
[20] *"Discours sur L'inégalité."* The translation is taken from C. E. Vaughan, *Studies in the History of Political Philosophy before and after Rousseau*, Manchester, 1939, I, pp. 172–173.

It is, in my view, impossible not to agree with these criticisms which apply with equal force to the Stoa, to St. Thomas, Hobbes, Pufendorff, Locke, Kant, and many others.

III

1. While this critique is valid, it is merely one of the various concrete systems of rights and duties deduced from natural law. It is not valid if it is leveled against the philosophical base of natural law. Every doctrine of natural law [21] is based upon the existence of man as a rational being who has an existence independent from the political society within which he lives. Only those who accept Platonism, Universalism, etc., can reject this basic truth. By speaking of man, we speak of him as being endowed with reason, for only thus can we define man (as contrasted with other forms of organic life). But if we accept the truth, then we do accept certain minima following from this proposition. These minima (and it is not important whether they are labeled natural rights or not) are thus valid, regardless of the political system, valid against any political system, even against a democracy.

This miminum can be enjoyed only by man—not by artificial persons such as corporations, states, etc.

i. These are the statements: the concrete content of the minimum is, first, the doctrine of the legal equality of all men. As man is rational, all men are rational. None can be enslaved. Not only the affected person, but every man, has the right to resist a law which aims at the enslavement of a part of mankind. The subject matter of the right is mankind, represented and manifested in each human being.

ii. All laws affecting life and liberty must be general in character. Individual laws are bills of attainder, constitute exceptional legislation, and violate the principle of equality. Resistance to them is thus legitimate.

iii. Retroactive laws, that is, *ex post facto* legislation depriving man of life and liberty, violate the principle of the law's universality. They are thus illegitimate, and resistance to them is legitimate.

---

[21] Except those purely "naturalistic" ones which allege the natural right of the stronger. See Plato in *Gorgias* (Callicles' statement).

iv. The enforcement of laws affecting life and liberty must be entrusted to an organ separated from the decision making agencies of the state. To this extent (but to this extent only) the doctrine of the separation of powers follows from proposition ii, namely, that laws infringing upon life and liberty must be general in character.

These four statements seem, in my view, to embody the minimum political content derived from the proposition of man's rational character. Not more. Violation of any of those four statements makes the exercise of political power illegitimate, and thus gives everyone (affected or not affected) a right to resist. Whether this right can prevail —is, of course, another matter.

2. This may sound very thin and unsatisfactory. But only if we forget that man may morally resist any command of his government if his conscience impels him to do so. This even Hegel recognized.[22] According to him, man's "inner voice" may well conflict with the precepts of positive law. This, however, is not a question of "right." There cannot be made a universally valid statement telling us when man's conscience may legitimately absolve him from obedience to the laws of the state. Every man has individually to wrestle with this problem. If he decides to resist, he cannot invoke a "right," but he will evoke our sympathy. Beyond the four statements on the unconditional right of resistance, each man must make his decision. Locke [23] and Hegel [24] agree that the strong state will be very lenient and tolerant toward those whose conscience makes it impossible to accept a state's orders. If it should not, the resister will, if his conscience urges him, resist and risk, rather than obey and be safe.

This dilemma between conscience and social order no theory can solve. If it pretends to do so, it will merely repeat abstract, empty formulae which, devoid of concreteness, merely veil the impossibility of squaring the circle.

With this note of skepticism I end.

[22] Note to preface to his *Philosophy of Right*.
[23] *Second Treatise* 11, Ch. XVIII, 208–209.
[24] *Philosophy of Right*. Note to § 270 (on Quakers and Anabaptists).

V

ON THE ENLISTMENT OF DUBIOUS ALLIES

BY

HANS SIMONS

I would like to qualify slightly the topic as assigned to me, because it seems to me that what we are discussing is the problem of loyalties, in my particular case loyalties in action and, therefore, a problem of the relationship between ends and means in practice. And I would like to emphasize these two aspects, because though I am not a trained philosopher, I am an educator, which means a man of practice, and that is the only field with which I am completely familiar. I say this because so many may feel differently.

Let me apologize at the very beginning that I am not going to contribute anything new or startling to this discussion. However, I think we still have to ask ourselves a basic question, namely, whether there is on principle a relationship between ends and means which can be defined? Does the end justify the means?

I am aware of the fact that there can be a logical answer, and that there is a moral answer to the problem; but I think we are living in a world where in practice we are utterly incapable of finding an answer.

The purgatory, for instance, is one of the worst examples of ends justifying means, surrounded as it is with an almost voluptuous imagination of torture and terror. Another is the death sentence. The best we can do is not to torture the fellow when we execute him.

Nor can we answer satisfactorily the problem of euthanasia.

Or take our own position in Western Germany, where within our own set of values we still adhere to the death sentence and apply it, while the Germans from a different point of view abolished it through an article in their Constitution, and now are resenting bitterly that we still use it.

Let me remind you of the war crimes trials, where for an end we used means which in themselves were, to say the least, questionable. We wanted to serve justice, but in order to do so we violated principles established in our own world, and we were left with at least a dubious result.

This confusion is by no means limited to the democratic world. The Soviet Union introduced the death sentence, then abolished it on principle, and then reintroduced it as a matter of expediency. It might well decide again that on principle it has to be abolished.

I think it is impossible to find an applicable principle clearly indicating the relationship between ends and means. We can turn the question around—logically there is no reason why we should not—and ask: Do the means justify the ends? What about certain practices in education, a topic not too far from your hearts. To what extent does education assume that its methods are sufficiently valuable to make the discussion of ends a matter of secondary concern?

How does our society regard the general relationship of action and effect within the setting of war? There are people who seriously insist that war is an opportunity for not only testing but developing the best virtues in man, and that it is worthwhile for that reason alone.

To take a less extreme argument: it is a fact that war solved to our satisfaction the problem of unemployment, and overcame the depression, which we could not master in any other way.

Today we are greatly improving our health services, as well as the techniques and the scope of our education, as part of our preparedness effort. One might argue that this alone justifies our emphasis on military strength.

To go completely away from the public into the private sphere: there hardly is a more dangerous means which is regarded as sanctifying the ends than selfish love. It is a very widespread type of love. As a matter of fact, it is the kind of love which our society encourages and admires.

Again I would draw the conclusion that there is no applicable principle which would establish a clear relationship between means and ends.

So we obviously have to satisfy ourselves with what one might call

On the Enlistment of Dubious Allies

relative standards, and I would like to mention a few. Is there, for instance, an overriding importance of one value which justifies forgetting about another one? Or are there priorities in the ends which would justify the dubious means used for their achievement?

Recently I read an article [1] which proposed very seriously and with excellent arguments that in order to solve the problem of population growth it would be necessary first to control the birth rate and during this period—which may be a long one, indeed—there should be no care for old people. For if we were to control birth and at the same time extend the life expectancy of the older generation, we would be left pretty much where we were. Therefore, it would be quite all right to let the old people die, while restricting the birth rate. This is a perfect instance of the dilemma presented by priorities in the values of ends.

Or look at Korea. A vast majority of Americans agree on the need for resisting aggression; but are we aware of the extent to which we are doing so at the expense of the Korean people? Is resistance to aggression the concept for which, in full agreement with us, Koreans would suffer what they have to suffer today? It seems difficult to reach agreement even on priorities. Not even a relative relationship between means and ends can be defined and stated.

If we cannot agree on priorities, perhaps we have prevailing attitudes. Are loyalties such that through them we can find a relationship between means and ends? I am personally very much concerned with one particular aspect of that problem, namely, the conflict between compromising for self-preservation, or becoming a martyr for a cause. I was in a position not so very long ago when I had the choice of either challenging National Socialism openly, or compromising to the extent of saving my own life. In the first case, I would have ended up in the corner of a concentration camp without anybody knowing much about it. In the other, I could get out and fight National Socialism from the outside. There are very strong arguments to be made on either side. Nobody who has not tried to make them for himself can know how irreconcilable they are.

Take, to come closer to home, the question of appeasement which

[1] Gerald Barnes, in *Antioch Review*, X, 4, pp. 445 f.

is nothing but a problem of compromise, a compromise for a cause, for instance, for the cause of survival of our country. I listen to the great debate which is supposed to be going on in this country. It may not be a great debate, but it certainly is lengthy. And you will agree with me there is again no answer on principle to the choice between the stubbornness of maintaining an attitude and the flexibility of compromising, in order to regain the freedom of action.

Turn to the problem of power. I do not know of any statement quoted as often and as uncritically as the one made by Lord Acton that power corrupts. I question it on its face value. But even assuming it is correct, we have not in our time developed a type of society which could possibly maintain order without authority and authority without power. Power, therefore, is essential. If it corrupts, then we have a dilemma for which we have no solution.

In other words, again I would conclude that there is no generally valid rule under which we could decide which of our attitudes are to prevail, and on which of our attitudes we should make our decision about what makes means and ends acceptable or permissible one for the other.

If this is a correct description of our situation, no wonder the world is confused. This confusion is not due only to the relationship between ends and means. It is also due to an added inconsistency in the use of means which is not even related to the discrepancy between means and ends.

What I mean is this: most of us have reached the point where we take a completely mechanical view of the use of social or political techniques. It is the gadget approach—even more common in this country than in countries less familiar with technology and less aware of its usefulness. As long as something works we think that is its justification, and we forget completely that beyond its mechanical working there may be other results. That leads to a misuse of techniques which while originally not a moral question becomes a problem of ethics for us.

We expect people to conform to our standards, because we are satisfied that they are superior. These very standards we try to spread, not by a process of consultation, agreements, and other democratic techniques, but by a method of imposition. On the other hand, the Soviet people are using democratic techniques, in order to establish a non-democratic end. Undoubtedly part of our confusion stems from the fact that it is so difficult to decide what the element of authoritarianism is in our efforts abroad, and of democracy in their practice of expansion. But we know that they are as little interested in the democratic end as we are interested in establishing tyranny.

Another and even greater confusion stems from the fact that ends are defined in terms of stages which already include alien, improper, inappropriate, or distorting means. Take a few instances which will clarify this point. The Soviet world lives under the plan, not yet completely realized, of the dictatorship of the proletariat, which is a technique to establish the classless society. If ever there was an end to which, defined in its stages, the means are more contradictory, I do not know of it. As for the West, we are now educating public opinion in the concept of a war for peace. It may be a preventive war, it may be a war we are forced into, it will hardly make for peace. Yet we try to convince ourselves that, however reluctantly, we fight only for an end which by definition is contradictory to the means suggested for it . . .

In this country, in particular, we are now waging a campaign where we are trying to impose conformity for the sake of freedom.

If there is anything incompatible with the essence of freedom, it is conformity. Yet we suppose that legislation, social pressures, or political investigations which impose conformity, will lead to the freedom which depends on diversity.

Behind this confusion a basic conflict confounds the problem. It consists of a state of enmity between different groups, which puts the enemy outside of the frame of reference within which each group tries to maintain its moral standards and its personal and collective loyalties. In this case, it is not the end which justifies the means, it is the enemy who does so. Consider again the attitudes and principles of the Soviet Union. The Soviet Union excludes a part of the world from the application even of its own moral standards. These moral standards may be alien and strange to us, but they exist. It would be a great mistake to say that the Soviet system is immoral by definition, but quite clearly within its morality the capitalists, the warmongers, the Western imperialists are not included. The West as the enemy justifies deceit, lawlessness, violence, and everything else which in our terms is unbearable and ununderstandable.

How about ourselves? Certain people found the most satisfactory justification for the use of the atomic bomb in their own attitude which excluded the enemy from the frame of reference within which they maintained moral attitudes. Our present security act legalizes such elimination of the enemy from the common standards of the country. Because certain things which are admittedly not within the tradition of America apply only to a definable enemy who is outside of the realm of our common agreement, they seem acceptable. Again it is the enemy, rather than the end, which justifies the means.

Sometimes loyalties as well as moral standards, like party politics, end at the water's edge. In such instances, the realm to which certain attitudes are not applicable is purely geographical. I would never be able to understand certain occupation morals which I observed for two and one-half years in Germany, if I were not convinced that people refuse to carry their standards beyond the frontier. This is true geographically. It is also true psychologically. For there are certain situations into which we refuse to carry standards, and where we take a moratorium on the relationship between means and ends. A civil war, for instance, is characterized by the abandon with which this relationship is disregarded.

A revolution usually brings about a situation where nobody cares any longer about the preparation of means and ends within a common concern. As a matter of fact, the character of the present world struggle as a sort of worldwide civil war of which the power conflict is only a part, makes it easier to understand why antagonisms are so violent and why the enemy is excluded from the application of one's own moral standards. The evidence suggests once more that it is impossible to solve these contradictions in practice.

It took me a long time to come around to the topic of my discussion, but these remarks are, I think, essential to it.

Dubious alliances are alliances where a relationship between ends and means cannot be clearly established. We are satisfied today to take as an ally anybody whom we regard as reliably anti-Communist. This, of course, is a choice by way of negative elimination. The litmus paper reacts both to acid and alkali. Politics, as Secretary of State Acheson sees the problem, makes only one distinction. This eliminates the whole area of attitudes between a reaction for and a reaction against—it calls on primitive and crude loyalties to the detriment of finer devotions. In addition, narrow loyalties prevent people from developing wide loyalties. We choose allies in terms of their social acceptability. We like people better when some of our standard notions fit them, and some of our standard values can easily be applied to them. This is one reason why we rely so heavily on the conserving and protecting attitude of the church in countries with which we are dealing. It is why wherever we go we fall in almost automatically with the "capitalists." Everyone abroad deals with the people with whom he would most easily connect at home.

Quite obviously Americans today are more interested in maintaining authority than in reshaping the forms under which it is established. This *status quo* attitude is insufficient and, therefore, dangerous in a changing world. Because of it neither the church nor capitalism nor conservative authoritarianism are reliable in terms of anti-Communism.

It is different where we pick our allies in terms of our own preference, but beyond the small loyalties of our class, of the people with whom we would like to associate. In terms of our larger loyalties we are allies of democracy and freedom. Here, too, we get immediately into trouble. What kind of democracy do we mean which we want to protect abroad? Most Americans think of democracy almost exclusively in terms of their own way of life. This for them is the best way of life for America. But is it also the best way of life for every other part of the world? We find it hard to accept the fact that Britain is a democracy. Personally I think it is even a better democracy than ours. In any case it certainly is a democracy, not a country where collectivism has extinguished individual freedom. We find it very hard to realize that the rest of the free world, while interested in the power of the United States for the sake of its own independence, is not primarily interested in defending our kind of democracy. As a matter of fact, we expect of our allies a sort of pro-Americanism comparable to the pro-Sovietism which Communism exacts all over the world.

Much evidence points in the direction of an increasing criticism of American democracy as it affects the rest of the world. The same can be said of freedom. Freedom for whom? Do we invite the rest of the world to fight for freedom in general? If so, what is it? Do we invite the rest of the world to fight for American freedom? Then what do they care? Do we invite the rest of the world to fight for its own freedom? If so, then how are we going to help to protect it? These are questions which American foreign policy has not even begun to answer, but which have to be answered before we can be sure that we get the right kind of allies.

Another difficulty is that our alliances are exclusively with governments. We have not, in spite of the Voice of America, and in spite of the great American tradition, succeeded in addressing ourselves to the peoples. I do not mean that like the Soviets we should try to establish Fifth Columns, or talk to peoples over the heads of their governments. That is not necessary. However, we certainly should avoid the impression which now is prevailing, that the only people we can talk to are the people in authority, and the only people we will deal with are the representatives of established governments. It can be done, and done very simply, as can be seen from just a few instances.

When Secretary of State Acheson went to Europe and paid a visit to London and Paris, he made it a point to see personally in Bonn the Chancellor of the West German Republic. He did not visit either Brussels or The Hague or any of the other capitals of countries in Europe which had suffered terribly from German occupation. One need not ask the Dutch or the Belgians or the Danes or the Norwegians how they felt about this, because one can readily imagine it.

Our President had a visit from the Prime Minister of Great Britain and from the Prime Minister of France. Nobody here made an attempt on those occasions to express our respects for the peoples of these two countries who are making sacrifices far beyond the sacrifices we are expected to make—though, of course, the results are far less spectacular.

We have discussed aid to India as if it were exclusively a problem of politics, without any consideration of the sensibility, the pride, and the prestige, both of the Indian people and the Indian government.

In our military preparations we face another insoluble dilemma. There is no question that as a country and as part of the Western world we have to get militarily ready. Strength is not only a physical phenomenon. It has its more fundamental elements. Thus far we have failed to build up these elements of moral strength. The explanation for it is that confusion between means and ends which I described before. We have to build positions not only of strength but of actually applicable power. Mere material strength makes for arrogance and self-centeredness. These, in turn, are attitudes which in the long run are likely to be self-defeating. If it is true in a practical sense, that the meek shall inherit the earth, our disregard of the moral elements of strength is, to say the least, dangerous.

In one respect, public opinion is aware of this danger. It is in regard to the baffling problem of Germany and German rearmament. We approach it as if it were exclusively a technical matter. First of all we do not know what kind of German army we want. If we want a volunteer army, we shall get an army of former German National Socialists and ardent Nationalists. If we want a draft army, we shall get an army of the rough boys, because under the Constitution it is legal to refuse to bear arms, and plenty of young Germans will make use of that article. In such a process of self-selection the result will be less than satisfactory.

We do not know whether we want a German army which needs all the paraphernalia of a military establishment. We do know that if we get it, whatever we succeeded in reviving or re-rooting of German democracy will necessarily be killed.

In addition, I think that German rearmament is bad international politics. Here is the one danger against which all of Europe would unite in defense. By American action a common denominator would be found for the small nations of Eastern and Western Europe, even for Communism and democracy in Western Europe. Revulsion against and fear of German rearmament can become the great anti-American issue which the Soviets try to exploit.

It seems true then that an inconsistency between ends and means very often turns out to be self-defeating.

There is still another relationship between ends and means, a kind of disparity in which an end may defeat the means which are applied to accomplish it. The typical instance of this is the policy of the Soviet Union. There are plenty of people who think that the Soviets are superb diplomats, that their policies are as clever and consistent as they possibly can be. This is plain nonsense. It is on the historic record that the Soviets created all the dangers which they tried to prevent. Because they believed dogmatically in it they caused capitalist encirclement, strengthened capitalist resistance, and produced the distrust. Worse still, since things came out the way they predicted, they feel confirmed in their interpretation and dispensation of Marxism. It is true that means can distort the end, or that the wrong means can actually prevent the end from ever being achieved. An instance of this is our way of permitting personal and political distrust to develop in a kind of vicious circle. This starts right at the home. I was out of this country for two and one-half years, and when I came back I realized how distrustful even Americans have become, how we are looking—fortunately not over our shoulders as the Europeans did under their dictators—but how we are looking around, how we are watching our step and sometimes our neighbor, in order to find out whether it is conviction or compulsion which produces acceptable attitudes. That is not the whole story. Distrust is worldwide, and it creates distrust as an answer. We have placed ourselves in a situation where we cannot even compromise any longer, because we do not expect others to accept the arguments on which any such compromise could be achieved, but only the power pressure which makes it unavoidable. If there is anything wrong with strength, I think it is the poison of pressure which enters into any arrangement power provides.

The only thing we can perhaps do, in order to clarify the relationship between means and ends, is to strive for more appropriateness. This is a very cautious and colorless word, but I use it on purpose. First, more appropriateness of techniques. If we have a system of democratic techniques, if we believe in our capacity as a people ultimately to make up our minds and reach a decision, we should permit other people to do the same. We should give them the freedom to become independent agents. We should give them the choice even of regarding themselves as neutral, if that is what they want to be.

Second, appropriateness within a set of values. If we believe, as we do, that ultimately victory will come to freedom—freedom of self-development, freedom of self-decision, freedom of making use of opportunities, and freedom eventually of choosing between several alternatives, then we should not by our attitude impose upon the rest of the world the sole alternative of being either for or against us.

I think that a greater appropriateness of means used to ends on which we can agree, would give us two satisfactions, and they are not entirely unimportant. It would give us, first, the satisfaction of logical consistency which seems to be important to men as rational beings. One of the greatest weaknesses of our present policy, domestic and international, is its utter lack of consistency. It is such that the rest of the world cannot possibly know where we are going. Often it seems even we ourselves find it difficult to know.

Secondly, it would also provide us with an easier conscience, which should be important to moral man. This nation is seriously troubled by an uneasy conscience. An honest attempt to bring means and ends into more appropriate relations would give us a sense of consistency and a better conscience. This in itself would be a great boon both to ourselves and to our allies.

VI

ON "MAKING FRIENDS WITH THE MAMMON OF UNRIGHTEOUSNESS"

BY

LISTON POPE

According to the King James version of the Bible, Jesus admonishes his disciples, in the ninth verse of the sixteenth chapter of the Gospel according to St. Luke, "I say unto you, make to yourselves friends of the mammon of unrighteousness; that, when ye fail, they may receive you into everlasting habitations." Probably no text from the sacred scriptures of the great religions has been translated into American life so completely as this one. According to the usual popular interpretation of it, the verse advises us to cultivate close friendship with worldly riches. American culture has not been willing to stop at friendship; it has fallen madly in love with the mammon of unrighteousness.

There can be no doubt that economic pursuits and values are made of supreme importance in American culture. The business man is the prototype of the American; the millionaire is the symbol of success. We measure men by their possessions, and train them to serve and to secure mammon. We educate college students, by and large, for success in economic pursuits. Even men and women who enter the learned professions tend quickly to become tradesmen in viewpoint and purposes, bartering their services for the highest fee practicable; this generalization does not apply to a great many individual doctors and lawyers who retain professional outlooks, nor does it apply very well to clergymen and teachers—who have little hope of getting rich anyhow.

The status of a church is often appraised in terms of the magnificence of its edifice and the size of its budget. We appraise a school in terms of the amount of its endowment and the salary of its football coach. We are a race of adding machines; perhaps we each deserve Oscar Wilde's definition of a cynic, as one who knows the price of everything and the value of nothing. Our culture is less interested in rightly dividing the word of truth than in legally dividing grandfather's estate.

When we study the uses to which our money is put, we discover a corresponding emphasis on material values. We spend nearly three times as much on cosmetics as on private research; we spend billions of dollars on armies and arms and a few million dollars on a Point IV program to assist underdeveloped areas. We spend nearly all our money, as individuals and as a people, on items that minister to the body, and we give our pennies and nickels for the life of the mind and spirit.

A poet has taken some poetic license with us, but not very much, in describing the values we consider to make life worth living:

One day in 1938 a man climbed out on a window ledge
Twenty-three stories or so above the street and he wouldn't come back.
Come back, come back, they cried, please come back,
And they offered him a Hershey bar.
But he shook his head no.
They offered him a nickel-plated cocktail shaker and a subscription to
   Life. . . .
No, no, no, he said, no, no, no.
They offered him . . . the niftiest chorus girl in all New York.
So finally he jumped, and people spoke with a strange light in their
   eyes,
Saying, He was mad, I tell you, mad, mad.[1]

Interestingly enough, the chief theorists of the two most powerful social systems in the contemporary world, capitalism and Communism, agree that man is basically an economic creature, that economic motives are the most powerful in life and that proper economic arrangements comprise man's fundamental purpose. Capitalism and Communism disagree about the proper arrangements. But

[1] Walker Gibson, "Gotham," *Harper's Magazine*, April, 1943.

"Friends with the Mammon of Unrighteousness" 71

they agree in their basic estimate of man as primarily an economic being. In view of our deification of economic values, we derive special comfort from the scriptural admonition to make friends of the mammon of unrighteousness. By ingenious exegesis, we can extend the apparent meaning of that verse from Luke to cover almost any kind of economic acquisitiveness. Various American clergymen preached "the gospel of wealth," as Professor Ralph Gabriel has called it. In the decades just after the Civil War, Russell H. Conwell, a Baptist minister of Philadelphia, delivered his famous lecture, "Acres of Diamonds," more than six thousand times. Its basic theme can be stated succinctly: "To secure wealth is an honorable ambition, and is one great test of a person's usefulness to others. . . . Tens of thousands of men and women get rich honestly. But they are often accused by an envious, lazy crowd of unsuccessful persons of being dishonest and oppressive. I say, Get rich, get rich! But get money honestly, or it will be a withering curse."

On occasion the proclamation of the gospel of mammon has been rather cynical, with very little concern for proper sanctions or restraints. More often, the pursuit of mammon has been presented as simply an inescapable necessity in the life of even the most religious person or the most moral institution. If we are commanded to be gentle as doves, we must also be wise as serpents. If moth and rust do corrupt, and thieves break through and steal, the realistic man will purchase moth balls and build a moisture proof, thief proof vault. Life may be more than meat, and the body than raiment, but food and clothes are still necessary.

The accumulation of great wealth has often been defended as providing an opportunity for philanthropy. John Wesley put this argument in a famous admonition to his followers: "Get all you can. Save all you can. Give all you can." John D. Rockefeller, Sr., gave an accounting of his own stewardship when he told the first graduating class of The University of Chicago: "The good Lord gave me my money, and how could I withhold it from The University of Chicago?"

In diverse and ingenious ways we have sought to justify the American gospel of wealth, and have often quoted scripture for that purpose, especially the command to make friends of the mammon of unrighteousness.

As a matter of fact, our use of that particular statement of Jesus represents a gross misunderstanding of his meaning. The statement follows immediately after the parable of the unjust steward. Once upon a time, according to the Gospel of Luke, there was a trust officer who betrayed his trust, and thereby made many friends and even won the commendation of the man he had betrayed. As Jesus told the story, a certain rich man had a steward about whose competence and honesty he came to be suspicious. He therefore demanded that the steward make an accounting, prior to his dismissal. Facing the loss of his job, the steward craftily considered the various alternatives. He might get a job at manual labor, but he concluded that he was not "strong enough to dig"; having had a white collar job, probably his muscles and his taste for physical exertion had become soft. He toyed at least briefly with the possibility that he might beg, but concluded that it was beneath his dignity: how his lord's tenants and debtors would laugh if they saw their former tormentor in such straits!

In a great crisis, the steward formulated a plan to save himself. In its essentials, the plan employed the formula of Dale Carnegie, for the steward decided to win friends whom he could visit when unemployed. He called in the accounts entrusted to his care, and discounted them handsomely, encouraging the debtors to falsify the amounts of their indebtedness. To this one he gave a twenty per cent discount; to that one a fifty per cent saving. Doubtless he winked slyly at each grateful debtor, and said rather broadly, "Oh, it's nothing at all. You can return the favor sometime."

Thus far, the story is not unique or remarkable. It could be matched in the annals of almost any municipal government's department of public works, where "rake off" does not refer to disposal of leaves and "kick back" does not mean a protest. In more charitable mood, we might compare the dishonest steward with Robin Hood, who also despoiled the rich to the advantage of the poor; but Robin Hood was not serving his own interest primarily.

"Friends with the Mammon of Unrighteousness" 73

The story does become remarkable when it reports without further explanation that the man whose resources had been squandered so lavishly "commended the dishonest steward for his prudence." Obviously, Luke has left something out. It may be that the steward convinced his master that most of the debts were worthless anyhow, and that the collection of fifty or sixty per cent represented a shrewd settlement. Or it may be that the master did not really know that the bills had been discounted, and was glad only that the books were in such good shape; in the days before certified accountants, balancing the books was easier than now. Or it may be, though it strains credulity, that the rich man knew he had been fleeced, but admired the shrewdness of the operation; Luke virtually asks us to accept this interpretation by adding the moral: "For the children of this world are in their generation wiser than the children of light."

We are not told whether the steward really lost his job. Perhaps his employer was so impressed that he persuaded the steward to remain in his service and to employ his remarkable talents thenceforth to his employer's advantage. It has been said that it takes a thief to catch a thief, and there is a kind of honor and mutual admiration among thieves. I can imagine that a happy partnership ensued, and that the rich man became richer in proportion as the unjust steward became more unjust. For the children of this world are in their generation wiser, and generally richer, than the children of light.

But an even more extraordinary development follows. Luke says that Jesus pointed up the moral of this parable by saying to his disciples: "I say unto you, make to yourselves friends of the mammon of unrighteousness, that, when ye fail, they may receive you into everlasting habitations." Surely no more remarkable statement was ever attributed to Jesus. He seems to be saying, "Observe the methods of the unjust steward. Go thou and do likewise." But this is incredible: nowhere else does Jesus urge such positive concern for the acquisition of wealth, or suggest that friendship can be bought.

Various efforts have been made to explain the parable of the unjust steward and the relation thereto of the maxim about the mammon of unrighteousness. It has been argued that the latter bears no intrinsic relation to the parable, but belongs with the other miscellaneous statements about wealth which follow the parable. Luke was deeply concerned with the problem of avarice, and he inserted into his manuscript at this point various observations on the subject, without intending that they should be read in the light of the parable preceding them.

Another interpretation holds that the parable of the unjust steward was not designed to illuminate the problem of wealth at all. Its central point, rather, is the ability of the steward to meet a crisis successfully. If the children of darkness are able to save themselves in a great crisis, it is clearly possible for the children of light to find salvation. The children of light must be as clever and diligent, for *good* ends, as was the unjust steward for unworthy purposes; they must not use his dishonest methods, but they must watch his ingenuity.

These explanations do not really deal, however, with the particular verse from which our topic comes. It is in order to look more closely at that verse itself. It has generally been misinterpreted. The verse does not advocate friendship with money, as we generally assume. The better translation of it in the Revised Standard Version says, "Make friends for yourselves by means of unrighteous mammon." Luke puts the entire matter of mammon in perspective half a dozen verses farther on, "You cannot serve God and mammon." Nor does the verse advocate making friends with people who have money, as the King James translation suggests, when it says "Make to yourselves friends of the mammon of unrighteousness." Rather, the disciples were commanded to use money for eternal purposes—to be faithful in economic matters, but always as a means to imperishable ends.

The real point of the verse, then, is not the elevation of mammon to a place of high value, but its proper use for eternal purposes. This is the central teaching of most of the great religions on the question of wealth.

But this teaching has seldom been really normative in human affairs, and never less so than at the present time. Man being what he is, and life's necessities being what they are, we can be certain that friendship with the mammon of unrighteousness, and with persons plentifully endowed therewith, will continue to be a perennial human ambition and institutional necessity—until the time, if ever, when history moves beyond our present materialistic age and the primacy of economic values. We do not live now in eternal habitations, and very few are able to share the humble abode of St. Francis of Assisi. At worst, we are the people with many houses on whom Amos poured his scathing denunciations. At best, we are inhabitants of the suburbs of the City of God.

VII

THE HIROSHIMA ISSUE

BY

W. W. WAYMACK

"The substance of the universe is obedience and compliance; and the reason which governs it has in itself no cause for doing evil, for it has no malice, nor does it do evil to anything, nor is anything harmed by it."—Marcus Aurelius.

Or, as Enrico Fermi has put it, the atom is a most law abiding thing. Our troubles are not there.

I approach this task of reflection from the standpoint of the problem which your Institute has posed—"The problem of reconciling group loyalties with moral codes . . . a problem that is most acute for those who hold the most responsible positions." I approach it with the limitations which I cannot escape, and which Dr. MacIver has told me he would not have me try to escape. These, it may not be inaccurate to say, are those of "a perhaps typical layman, with probably the normal equivalent of conscience and humaneness, who happened for a couple of years to have had to live in some intimacy" with some of the problems loudly but unclearly announced to the world in 1945 at Hiroshima.

I start by saying that there are not any simple, neat, and easy answers to any of the almost innumerable problems involved. Everything calls for very hard thinking to ascertain real significances, and then for weighing and balancing to produce, all things considered, the wisest possible answers. The greatest simplicity that anyone is likely to find in any important aspect is a dilemma. More commonly it is a trilemma, a quadrilemma, or worse.

The first great job in preparing ourselves to face any part of the issue is education in the fact that we shall find only complexities, that grasping for simple and soul-satisfying answers that relieve us from strain is futile. Our experience so far has been characterized far too much by that.

This has been inevitable. It has been a natural consequence of the way the complex set of problems that we call "the issue" burst upon us.

But let us set out the central facts of the "Hiroshima Issue," think about them as objectively as we can, and try to discover the moral issues (the conflicts of loyalties) "through the realities and not over them." I think the pertinent questions are:

What is it that we have?

In what way did it come?

How have we behaved with respect to it?

What is its relation to other realities that minds and consciences must take account of?

How far can we push our understanding of the eventual significances, the deep and broad implications for a long tomorrow, of the new knowledge that presented us with the Hiroshima Issue?

None of the answers can be complete; but it is probably only essential that they be complete enough to show the significance of the questions.

What Is It That We Have?

Reserving the fact that we have far more than the atomic weapon, the weapon is the source of our issue, so I limit the question to that.

We have a new military explosive of fantastically increased power. So great is the stepping-up of the familiar effects of blast and heat that the quantitative difference has been called by some a qualitative difference, making obsolete all former values, including the moral. In addition, there is the unfamiliar effect of radioactivity, which in some possible uses of the explosive can be a major effect.

With this weapon, physical destruction can be compressed enormously as to time. This makes vastly more difficult the problem of countering the effects and it adds enormously to the danger of a surprise attack.

Methods of delivery to targets include primarily, as yet, the airplane, with other obvious possibilities such as launched missiles, short range and long range.

There is the further possibility of producing still more powerful "fusion" bombs, which might or might not be militarily advantageous. And any type of nuclear weapon can be so made and so used as to maximize radioactivity.

The nuclear weapon can be used "strategically" or perhaps "tactically" (in support of operations by other military forces). Used strategically, it is the most dramatic of the weapons of mass destruction. So used, the target can be cities and their populations, or can be more specific objectives, such as industrial concentrations of exceptional military importance. Even in the latter case, both the limitations of precision in delivery and the very nature of such industrial concentrations mean large scale killing.

It is essential to recognize two facts. First, this is a weapon "of a new order of magnitude," yet of definitely finite effect. Second, it is but one of the available and already used means of mass destruction, with other such means obviously possible. The "Hiroshima Issue," therefore, does not encompass, by any means, the problem raised by mass destruction, but is essentially only the symbol of it.

In What Way Did It Come?

The atomic weapon came through peaceful scientific research into the nature of nature. The practicability of it was an inevitable evolutionary development. This was but expedited by the war. We should have had to deal with it in time anyhow.

The expediting was done in secrecy, as far as publics were concerned. The success was revealed suddenly over Hiroshima and Nagasaki. Our people, our politicians in and out of office, our civil leaders of all kinds, and even our agencies of public information and education, were utterly unprepared to understand anything about it except its staggering destructiveness. In a vacuum as to understanding, there could be no general grappling with implications; there could only be awe, thought paralysis, frustration, a little of what some scientists called "a sense of sin," and a powerful tendency to generate and hug illusions. The anxious efforts of atomic scientists to educate were invaluable—as a start at moving mountains.

Thus, because of the way it was revealed, the revolutionary advance in scientific knowledge was bound to be received. And so it was.

How Have We Behaved with Respect to It?

The secrecy and suddenness dictated by war considerations were factors piled upon a grave general lack of understanding of science itself. The main price that we have had to pay so far is our inability to fit "the bomb" into its proper place in any field—warfare, technical evolution, social and political evolution, morals. If the development had come openly, therefore, by assimilable stages, like the airplane, even though this had been relatively fast, these problems would have been much less difficult. As it did come, we got generalizations ahead of facts, and are still in the resulting fog.

Nevertheless, the awe was not valueless. In the first year, post Hiroshima, it suppressed littleness and stimulated greatness. Though a very few really comprehended, America accomplished two splendid things. Wisdom and conscience were in them. We evolved and got committed to a program for international atomic energy control which, though it has proved impossible to put into effect, and though we now know it rested partly on some incorrect assumptions, was admirable both in motive and in enlightened vision. We also adopted domestically a controlling law for atomic energy development that, while it could not foresee everything and said so, was an outstanding legislative achievement.

We have also, however jerkily, in the subsequent four years reduced the appalling want of knowledge and of understanding substantially. Progress is by no means sufficient, but it marches.

But the want of understanding has meantime done mischievous work, too. Driven by unpleasant realities of the "cold war," men have

The Hiroshima Issue

grasped at deceptive simplifications of complex realities and irrational identification of Security with Secrecy alone and narrowly defined, at illusions of the "Maginot Line" variety, at the notion that hostile espionage can be dealt with only by jettisoning our basic values. Sometimes men have exploited fear and suspicion for purposes less than noble.

All this we still have with us. It is an obstacle alike to authentic national security and to morality. It is full of "conflicts of loyalties." And it is part of the Hiroshima Issue.

How Does the Issue Relate to Other Realities That Minds and Consciences Must Take Account Of?

Consideration of any new weapon is bound to be fruitless, unless it is in relation to the nature of modern war and to the facts which determine this. The two main facts are these:

1. The long process by which men resistlessly join in ever larger political and social unities has brought us to the stage of a two camp world. The loyalties of men, often ferocious, have been transferred progressively from tribe and city-state, and, in an important degree, from religion, to the nation-state and to vast imperialisms of changing forms. There is a reaching toward worldwide unity, but the stage is the two camp stage. A major war, therefore, is a worldwide war.

2. The industrial age has made war a struggle not between champions (a David and a Goliath), nor between small professional armies, but between whole organized peoples, especially their productive "economies." It has both made "productive capacity" the vital factor and provided means of attacking productive capacity. The inexorable adaptation of war to the industrial age and its products, has destroyed the old distinction between combatants and noncombatants. It has not only brought new weapon after new weapon, but it has also determined that the use of older weapons shall be more "indiscriminate."

Each new weapon—musket, submarine, airplane, atomic bomb—has horrified people and has inspired attempts to proscribe it. None that promised effectiveness has ever been foregone. Each novel application of old kinds of force, dictated by the character of the age, has similarly produced a wave of revulsion but has similarly, if effective, become part of accepted strategy. For instance, the blockade or siege, directed not at a garrison in a fortress but at a population in a besieged nation makes no distinction between combatant and non-combatant; it is thoroughly indiscriminate. The shift in the primary use of submarines from the sinking of warships to the destruction of commerce was shocking in 1914–1918, an unchallenged method in 1939–1945. Use of bombing planes in the past war, prior to Hiroshima, is another example.

Mass destruction both of property and lives, at which an "unenlightened" Genghis Khan, with minimum armament, was not incompetent, has become part of modern war with the weapons available now. There is essentially no difference, except in substituting a few hours for a few months, in what happened at Hamburg and Tokyo, on the one hand, and what happened at Hiroshima and Nagasaki on the other. Mass destruction, not the means of it, is the horrifying thing. It can be and has been accomplished by means ranging from the primitive to the most complicated mechanical devices. Restraints upon it, in any war that comes, will be only those dictated by whatever motivates men carrying the awful responsibility of decisions on the two hostile sides. As no normal human loves destruction for its own sake, any war waged by any people, including a people so essentially humane that it abhors destruction, enforces action on the principle that the end justifies the means. Real restraints upon means, therefore, given leaders as compassionate as Lincoln, will be dictated by the nature of the end, and by the success that men can have in keeping ends foremost.

No man of decent instincts who has had any responsibility for atomic weapons will be calloused as to what they can do. A great deal of narrowness or a great deal of hate would be required for that.

But the realities of modern war are hard and brutal things. The true problems for the moral sense, the really significant conflicts of loyalties, are not to be found in brooding over a particular weapon exclusively.

The Hiroshima Issue

The significance of the Hiroshima Issue is in what it leads intelligent minds to. It is the dramatic illumination of what modern war has become. Mass destruction by whatever means is indeed horrible. Even that is not the basic issue. What men must face is the question of purposes, moral purposes. The evil of war itself can be justified only by the presence of greater evil for which it is the only alternative. For those who say with deep sincerity that there can be no greater evil, I have respect. It is clear that they do not prevail in the world. For most of us, our final loyalties go to values for which we would fight—and which we would desperately want the fighting to preserve and advance.

The more we recoil from mass destruction in war, the more we must recoil from war. The more we recoil from war, the more we will find the greatest immorality in the thinking, the policies and the actions that move the world toward war.

We of this land have not been free from fault, of course; though for the most part we honestly do not know where we have done badly. As a people we have not wanted to do so.

I believe the real issue in the world today is between tyranny and individual freedom, as it has been through the ages. I do not for a moment think that this is a mere shibboleth, a rationalization of nationalist patriotism. It was true before there were nation-states, and will be true when nation-states have vanished.

We are a people of compunctions. All democracies based on the liberal philosophy are largely governed by compunctions. Our propensity for them may confuse and mislead us sometimes. But the phenomenon is our greatest glory.

In the end, the moral issue always goes to the nature of ideas, to the theories that men hold, to the philosophies that dominate them and that they would press upon others. If men have compunction about the methods that they may use to make their concepts prevail, it is because of the quality of the concepts; and if they have no compunction about methods, that also is because of the quality of the concepts. Ours always trouble us and can even be used to weaken us sometimes. But they stem from our philosophy and they are the ultimate proof of its nobleness.

Compunctions appear for us not only in relation to warfare. All our social behavior is shot through with them—our Bill of Rights, our restraints upon the holders of power, even when the holder of power is a majority of all of us. It may be true—I think it is—that the reason for our basic method of self-restraint is that we are never sure we have at a given moment all the answers. And that unsureness is a correct reflection of our fundamental idea.

We know where we want to go, toward justice in all its applications. We conceive of justice as not a material concept alone, but also a spiritual. We believe it must free the minds and souls of men, of men individually, one by one. How to achieve this justice we never quite know, we know that we do not know, and we are convinced that it is not given to any other group of men to know, far in advance, with sureness. Hence our conviction that finding answers is inevitably a piecemeal business, that it requires freedom of the individual mind and spirit, that restraints and compunctions limiting the powerful are not only generous but essential. Hence our belief that morals and methods are inextricable.

The Communist philosophy, like ours, began in idealism and aimed at a heaven on earth. The purposes of the Bolshevik conquerors of power in Russia were doubtless of that sort. However complicated by other motives now, nationalist and personal, I assume that the Kremlin masters still consider themselves the carriers of salvation. The horrible wrongness is in their arrogant assumption that they and they only have all the answers, or the infallible formula of dialectical materialism by which any needed answer can be produced on the instant. This appalling, deadly sureness produces their scorn for the notion that morals have any place in methods. It determines the nature of their tyranny. It includes forcing into the mold that they prescribe or devise every significant factor of human life—from political expression to musical, from the factual discoveries of the natural sciences to the right of a man to incubate a thought.

When those for whom means and morals have no relation, because they alone have the tablets on which the future is graven and the undiluted right to help it happen, when these men suddenly develop an interest in the morality of means which others may use to resist them, it is time to be on guard. It is not that we should be ashamed of our own compunctions. It is that we should face the issue of morality complete, that we should not permit a sense of moral dilemma that does us proud to be made a moral trap. The devious and twisting worldwide propaganda campaign against the atomic bomb is clearly an effort to make it that.

One of the "fission products" of Hiroshima, in the field of attitudes and not foreseeable, is the issue raised by some with their justification of "preventive war." The limitations, arising out of moral sense, that are self-imposed in liberal democracies are well illustrated by this. There is the moral recoil from striking first. We might with reasonable humility remember that this recoil from taking the aggressive militarily for anti-aggressive reasons has heretofore been easier for us than for, say, a democratic people in continental Europe. It has been genuine morality with us, but one which heretofore we have never seriously doubted that we could afford.

Despite the changed conditions, despite the case that can be made for at least intercepting and destroying an attack already launched against us (the Pearl Harbor example), I think the great majority of our people are right in their moral judgment that initiating world war with its incalculable consequences is something we cannot do.

Peace is a value to which all profess loyalty. Peace, to be sure, is but opportunity, and the essence of its value is in what we do with the opportunity. But war is so largely uncontrollable in its consequences that he whose policies obviously bring it closer is surely guilty of terrible immorality. If that applies to "preventive war," it surely applies to calculated aggression.

And I suggest that in any time, and especially in our time, when in a two camp world the contest is truly "for the minds of men," the "immorality" that our humane consciences are asked to attach to a particular weapon would well be amplified a thousand times and directed to the policy of the Iron Curtain. The so-called "closed system," which is a denial of access to understanding, is, from every moral standpoint that I can comprehend, indefensible.

In the test that humankind, at this stage of its evolution, faces, there are many hard choices between greater and lesser evils.

Beyond Weapons and War

How far can we push our understanding of the eventual significances, the broader and deeper implications for a very long tomorrow, of the new knowledge that, in something less than a micro-second, presented us with the Hiroshima Issue?

If by "Hiroshima Issue" we mean not merely the impact upon politics of a new weapon of terrible power, but rather the whole impact of the revolution in scientific thought which the weapon tragically dramatized, the full significance of it is beyond appraisal.

What mankind knows or thinks it knows in any age about the structure and mechanics of the universe, about natural forces and how they work, about the possibilities and limitations of man's own observations of them, affects everything in the realm of ideas, comprehension and apprehension, philosophy and religion, and all.

Who even now can measure all the effects of the Copernican revolution upon thought, faith, and institutions?

Who doubts that Newtonian physics had great effects on thoughts and trends in human affairs far beyond the range of observable and measurable physical phenomena? . . . Objective time . . . Objective space . . . A mechanistic universe subject to natural laws, all sharply determinable and the major ones apparently discovered . . . Man and his mind as a spectator and scrutinizer presumably capable of finding the true cause-and-effect relationships in any phase of environment.

How much of encouragement to materialism, even to the religion of dialectical materialism, flowed quite unintended from the advances of physical knowledge presented to man by the Newtonians?

And now the neat and final completeness of all that is gone. The Newtonian discoveries were enormously useful. But they represented a stage, not finality. The premises of post-Newtonian thinking no longer exist. The concept of relativity has destroyed them. This concept I, like most laymen, can but dimly understand; yet its shattering effect is obvious. . . . Mass and energy have their equivalence. . . . One can become the other, and in certain conditions does. . . . The process of creation goes on continuously, along with the process of running down. The physics of the nucleus of the atom was not foreseeable through the old knowledge. It has been approachable through the new, as to some things even predictable. And to that the episode of Hiroshima, which troubles us so much, is but a footnote.

It will be for human minds a long time hence to assess, probably as feebly and uncertainly as we assess the past, the effect upon humankind of the new bases of scientific understanding that the half century has brought.

Having recognized the impossibility of confident appraisal, I shall be guilty now of the usual human presumption, the kind in which the finite calls upon the infinite to support the notions that it finds comfortable.

I confess (and confess is the word) that all the little fragments of knowledge that I pick up, including those contributed by science, about the way the universe is put together, preach to me of two things. They preach to me of diversity. And they preach to me of unity. Two principles, it seems to me, that are observable everywhere. The more we manage to observe, the more so. And the next discernment, I think or I think I think, is the phenomenon of equilibrium. It keeps apparent opposites from canceling out. It is, or appears to be, the ordering factor.

That seems to be so in astro-physics. It seems to be so (and here is the leap) in the relations of man to man. I grasp at the universality of it to bolster my notion, comfortable to me, that only the one applied philosophy of human relations that in its very essence allows for balance of opposites, can possibly fit human destiny. I know of no applied philosophy which does this, or tries to, except the kind which we call ours though it is ours only as the fruit of the past.

And it seems to me that the forms of diversity, in the unfolding story of men, change in a way that fits an evolutionary pattern. It seems to me that the scope of unity changes, and that the pattern is clear there, too.

And loyalties, which are the emotional, perhaps the spiritual, cement of unities, gradually change in accordance.

We of today shall hardly see the transfer of even the major loyalties to the unity that is the concept of the Brotherhood of Man. But, grim as is a world divided into two, with nuclear-reaction devices of persuasion substituted for clubs, we are closer.

The "IF" that is involved, and that we are all sufficiently troubled by, the one that could set us back for centuries, hardly requires stressing.

VIII

INSTITUTIONALISM AND THE FAITH

BY

LOUIS FINKELSTEIN

One of the most curious and significant traits distinctive of man, as contrasted with all other forms of life, is his concern with institutions. Man has been defined as the thinking animal, the laughing animal, the toolmaking animal, the animal with tradition and culture, the animal with imagination and purpose. Yet his history has been most profoundly affected by his character as institution builder. His future may depend far more on the manner in which he uses his institutions, than on any other aspect of his creativeness. Institutions are his foremost danger and promise. They, not gadgets, will decide his fate.

In institutions, the individual becomes enlarged, and frequently he develops a passion for his institutions far greater than his love for himself. Indeed, the institution is often for him a nobler self, justifying martyrdom for its sake. Obviously, the oldest institution is the one which has its roots in prehuman biological evolution, namely, the family. In primitive life, the family or clan generally outranks the individual as focus of his attention. Man faces his own death with some equanimity; he is far more disturbed at the prospect that his family or clan might perish.

It is clear that together with the aggressiveness which man has inherited from prehuman ancestors, he has also inherited a desire to serve. The clan and family are ideally suited to satisfy both needs. The individual serves a cause beyond himself; he does not have to defeat his aggressiveness, however; all he has to do is to project it on the institution, and seek for it a status in a pecking order of clans, such as individuals, in lower forms of life, seek for themselves.

A remarkable passage in the first chapter of Genesis seems to take cognizance of this aggressiveness which the individual projects on his family or clan, and to suggest a manner of dealing with this aggressiveness which will prevent it from leading to mass destruction. The passage anticipates in many ways William James's concept of the Moral Equivalent for War.

Adam, having been created, is told to "be fruitful and multiply, and replenish the earth, and subdue it; and have dominion over the fish of the sea, and over the fowl of the air, and over every living thing that moveth on the earth." Man's aggressiveness is to be directed against animate nature, rather than against his fellows within the individual tribe. The whole world, being descended from Adam, is to regard itself as a single family or clan, in which all are for one another, as they might be in the closely knit primitive kinship group. There is to be no pecking order within the human group, whether among individuals or among clans. All are equally the bearers of the Divine image. Man's search for dominion and his need for submissiveness and belonging can both be satisfied, through developing the same passion for mankind, that one feels for one's family; and through a search for control of Nature rather than one's fellow man.

Realization of this ideal, foreshadowed so early in the history of civilization, eludes man; there has been no large aggregation which has for any length of time fulfiled the direction of the Book of Genesis in this respect. The history of man is, on the contrary, one of the rise of new and larger institutions—the tribe, replacing the clan; the nation, replacing the tribe; the empire, replacing the nation. But always there is a group of men who are outside the kinship group, and over whom the inside group feels it may rightly seek domination.

In urban life, loyalties which were associated with primitive clan, family, and tribal organizations are transferred not only to the state or empire, but to smaller voluntary organizations, such as professional and trade groups, schools, trade unions, and baseball teams. The hunger for pre-eminence for one's college or school, the pride in

Institutionalism and the Faith

the victory of one's favorite team, the astonishing passion aroused in connection with a football game or boxing match, are all significant of the survival of a pecking order among men; and of the projection of the impulse for precedence on institutions, instead of kinship groups. In the transitional stages of human history, indeed, such institutions as guilds disguise themselves as clans or families, in order that they may possess loyalties similar to those which primitive man associates with his institutions. Fictional ancestors are invented to transform what would in our day be a simple guild into a clan, with origins in an ancient, forgotten past.

In our time, institutional aggregates have become larger and more powerful than ever. They are no less competitive than in the past; and in their political and economic forms seem to threaten the future of the human race, or at least civilization, with complete destruction.

The evil of institutionalism which is particularly obvious when it takes the form of imperialism and warlike aggression, is by no means limited to those vast aggregates of power. A condition which makes the rise of such gigantic forces of destruction possible, is the less easily observed institutionalism which pervades the general culture. One reason, for example, that colleges and universities are but moderately effective instruments for the development of wiser and better men, is that they are engaged in such ceaseless rivalry as to leave them no leisure to think through the common problems of mankind. Management and labor, together, might build a democratic economy, both secure and dynamic, but spend their energies in a hundred battles, exhausting their best intellectual and moral energies. Almost all our cultural power is thus used in unproductive friction. This fact, probably more than any other, accounts for the failure of *homo sapiens* with his Western culture to make his national and international organizations effective instruments for the attainment of his own goals.

Institutionalism is a significant phenomenon even in regard to the smallest organizations the modern world develops. A letterhead with a title creates loyalties in the minds of some, and works enormous havoc with rational thinking.

In the course of a life which has involved a good deal of institutional activity, I have often found this astonishing loyalty to a name overriding all clarity of judgment, and even purity and propriety of behavior. Men commit transgressions on behalf of institutions which they would never commit for themselves. Men are cruel in their efforts to save the institutions to which they have devoted themselves, as an animal might be ruthless in the protection of its young. I have known men very generous toward their employees, but harsh in their treatment of employees of their synagogue or church. They seemed to be far more concerned lest the religious institution invade its capital, than lest they invade their own! My mother once remarked to the president of a congregation who was overconcerned for the financial security of the institution he headed, "My friend, I am sure that the congregation will survive both of us. Let us not transgress the law of generosity to protect it." She was right. She and the president of the congregation have both long gone to their eternal reward; the congregation still exists, and doubtless has still those who would violate many commandments for the sake of its supposed good.

If all institutionalism were of this rabid and diseased form, the future of man and his civilization would be bleak and dreary, if not hopeless. The only manner in which man can be redeemed in an age of cultural complexity is through institutions; for it is institutions which must translate ideas into effective action. Fortunately, the message of Genesis has not been entirely wasted. In the great religions of mankind, there is a persistent effort to persuade man to transcend all desire for pre-eminence over his fellows in any manner, and to seek a brotherhood in which all will be equal before God. The burden of all religious teaching is that existence and life have a meaning and purpose beyond themselves, and beyond all temporal existence; that the individual, and all the institutions he creates, are justified in so far as they contribute to the fulfilment of that meaning and purpose; that no institution can be both finite and the goal of earthly striving, but only a means toward that goal. Hence it follows that primitive man was in error in attributing to his clan or tribe an absolute significance; and we are in equal error in attributing absolute significance to any of the institutions in which we find our visible and tangible fulfilment.

Institutionalism and the Faith

Obviously, the task of lifting men's sights, so that they feel loyalties not to part of creation but to the Creator, and see the goal of existence not in institutions but in that which institutions themselves serve, falls on religion. The perfection of man's character can come only when he develops this longer vision; and this longer vision can come only through institutions which are created for that purpose.

This task ought not to be utopian. There is no need for transforming human nature, or even the basic impulses of our culture. No such transformation occurred when men substituted national for tribal loyalties, or imperial loyalties for national ones. The Americans of the latter part of the eighteenth century developed a loyalty to their country, which transcended that to their states, without any transformation of character.

The message of Genesis is precisely this. The task of human redemption for peace and cooperation is not one of basic change but of broadening vision. In this very symposium, Professor Harold D. Lasswell tells us that the world has become a village, in certain respects, most of them unsatisfactory. The question is whether it can come to possess also the advantages of village life.

The main obstacle, it seems to me to this reorientation and reeducation of man is that there is no one to undertake it. Religious institutions to which the task is congenial and natural, like other institutions, consist of men and women. They are themselves children of our present culture and state of mind.

Even though their heads reach into the heavens, their feet are planted on the earth. The primitive and pagan deification of the family and clan finds its counterpart not only in similar deification of colleges, universities, nations, and empires, but also of religious institutions themselves. In the necessity of developing religious loyalties, writers and religious statesmen frequently find it easier to appeal to man's impulse to hate the stranger, rather than to his impulse to love his neighbor. It is easier to unite against, than to unite for; especially when the opposing force is visible and human, and the uniting goal is distant and abstract. In trying to awaken men's love for forgotten martyrs, religious writers often, unintentionally perhaps, arouse even greater animosity toward those who persecuted the martyrs. Most

Jews (to speak of the members of my own faith) remember that Titus burned the Temple; fewer know that Rabban Johanan ben Zakkai built the academy of Jabneh partly to replace it. Everybody thinks of Hitler with horror; very few even know the name of Leo Baeck, who, having endured years at Theresienstadt, emerged an even greater saint and scholar than when he entered.

Religious institutions may be strengthened by the recollection of the saintliness of martyrs or of the cruelty of those who tortured them. To do the first, requires, however, much greater ability and training than the second; because it seems that man's reaction to hostility lies nearer the surface of his mind and spirit than his reaction to affection.

Every religious institution, as Dr. Bryson reminded us some time ago, tends to contain two groups both in its leadership and in its following. There are those to whom the real task of religion is uppermost and who find themselves more akin with the truly religious of other denominations and sects than with the semi-religious or irreligious of their own. There are also those whose religion is really a kinship loyalty to their own denomination or sect, and whose primary loyalties are directed toward it. For them, religious organization is not different in kind from temporal and political organization.

In an age which measures effectiveness by popularity and achievement by size, it is obvious that the latter group will be identified with real religious leadership and widely admired. For in the nature of things, and for reasons which have been mentioned, such men can attract numbers, not available to the teachers of true religion. With the vast growth in power of instruments of propaganda, the "denominationalists," as we may call the men of religion whose primary interest is the welfare of their group and institution, are likely to appear to have an increasing advantage over the religionists, as we may call those whose primary interest is the service of God and the betterment of human character, and who regard their institutions themselves as means toward that greater goal.

Quite aside from this patent fact, there is a spiritual and moral perplexity which confronts the religionists, and sometimes prevents them from being as effective as even their small numbers and the difficulty of their task might permit. They have to face the need of

Institutionalism and the Faith

maintaining their institutions, in order that the greater goals might be served. They understand that the institutions are not ends but means. Yet by what logic and eloquence can they impart to their followers and prospective followers at once a passion for institutions, as instruments to serve God, and at the same time, an objective appraisal of their relative rather than absolute role in culture? In an age of exaggerated institutional claims, how shall we proceed to build institutions on precision and accurate statement of the truth?

The problem of religious leadership is essentially similar to that which confronts conscientious statesmen, who have come under the influence of religion. In a world which threatens men with conflict, national loyalties may well decide the issue. Yet statesmen under the inspiration of men of religion, ancient and modern, have established the United Nations. To fly the flag of the United Nations is a gesture which both expresses and fosters loyalty to mankind at large. It seems to many that this loyalty will necessarily help undermine the will not only to war, but also to resist aggression; and they see in the flag of the United Nations a peril to their own state. Yet to fail to accept the flag of the United Nations as a symbol of human unity, is to court frustration of the ultimate purposes of mankind.

Perhaps, awareness of this dilemma of statesmen and politicians may help us think more clearly of our problem as teachers of religion. Clearly we should advise political leaders that they must accept the risks involved in the instruction of the world in international and transnational unity, and overcome the fears and anxieties which are associated with such instruction. It requires subtlety to appreciate both the need to defend the nation and the need to foster international brotherhood. It requires great faith in God and in mankind, daringly and boldly to strive at once for the distant goal of human political unity, and to appreciate the immediate necessity and indispensability of national security.

The challenge which confronts men of religion is likewise essentially one of faith. Solomon Schechter, who was the person most responsible for the reorganization of The Jewish Theological Seminary of America in its present form, used frequently to say to those in perplexity, "You must leave a little bit to God." I believe that men of religion would be more likely to escape confusion and error in their problems of institution *versus* goals of institutions, of means *versus* ends, if they could bring to the problems of their work, the faith they preach so eloquently to others.

Essentially our dilemma is that of Jeremiah, who, devoted to the Temple of Jerusalem with passion of which the priests of that Temple could know nothing, still had to spend much of his time declaring that the Sanctuary—important and significant as it was—was only the house of God, and not God Himself. Perhaps the fate which awaits those who hold these views is that which came upon Jeremiah—to fail so far as their own time is concerned—but they cannot fail so far as the future of man is concerned.

A way must be found to develop a consciousness of the common goals which all men of true religion have before them, so that together they can overcome the recurrent threats of paganism. We cannot in an age when division among men spells not only continued spiritual immaturity but even physical and cultural destruction, further postpone the fulfilment of our duty to rear a generation of religionists, rather than institutionalists. If religious institutions could not be built on the foundations of human love and cooperation, the future would be so bleak that the institutions themselves would be worthless. It may require redoubled energy and great sacrifices on the part of all of us, delay in the time we have set for the fulfilment of our programs, diversion of effort from immediate to long range goals. But the truth cannot be taught through falsehood, and the God of Scripture cannot be worshiped in the form of a golden calf.

The basic truth of religion is that of Jeremiah, and not of the false prophets who opposed him. The sanctity of the Temple resided not in its bricks, but in its transcendent purpose. Even institutions of religion cannot without danger to their real ends, pursue goals of power and domination. As they show other institutions examples of cooperativeness and vision, they may hope for true success and for justification of their efforts.

Those who hold to this truth find themselves burdened with the heaviest of tasks, to develop in their coreligionists the deeper in-

Institutionalism and the Faith

sights needed to win them to the doctrine of cooperation and affection across differences of background, traditions of hostility, and histories of conflict; while at the same time they must labor, like others, for the advancement, as well as spiritual perfection of the institutions themselves. There is no escape from this double service. All we can be certain of is that "though there be delay, we may hope for Him."

Perhaps it is easier to transcend institution-mindedness in this generation than it could have been in any other, for it is clear that, in fact, man has no alternative. Jeremiah's words carried a conviction to those with eyes to see, because no one could doubt that the alternative was not only the doom of the Temple, but destruction of all hope for its re-establishment. No one can tell today whether or not we have lost the present; in any event, there is not much we can do about it. We cannot over night create a statesmanship capable of handling the perplexities of our time, and citizenry able to understand them. But whether the present can be saved or not, there can be little doubt of our duty and the importance of saving the future, should we escape current terrors. Whatever may be the outcome of the present and immediate conflicts in the world, there will be a future generation which will need the insights religion has offered for these hundreds of generations, and which will escape its perils, in the light of those insights. The task of statesmen is to deal with the immediate; that of the religious teacher with the distant and the eternal. The distant and the eternal require cothinking, cooperation, and mutual respect among religious individuals and institutions. The time has come when religious people cannot fulfil themselves, except by being truly religious. They can serve at all, only by determining to serve God.

No one can read the newspaper headlines in our day without increasing conviction that religion and its outlooks contain the only hope for the modern world. But to fulfil that hope, modern religion must be religious. Its institutions must rise above institution-mindedness. Its leaders must be able to serve the God, Whose love transcends all differences, and in the love of Whom man can distinguish no differences. The survival and growth of the civilization of which all of us are part will thus be determined by the reality and depth of its commitment to true religion.

If there is no hope for civilization outside of religious commitment which transcends mere denominationalism, it is clear that there is little hope for the survival and advancement of any of our faiths, without such commitment. Denominationalism itself, therefore, demands that we transcend it; just as true patriotism in our time must be international as well as national. It may be given to a small number of men, who realize the great peril and challenge of the day, to meet it, to interpret it to their fellows, to help raise the sights of mankind, so that the very danger will become a means for the betterment of the race. It seems probable that religious teaching has never had so great a hold on men, as it has today; and also that never before has it been in such great peril. Great achievement and unprecedented opportunity for service are available for those who grasp this truth, and are the first to develop institutions, which serve, rather than seek to dominate.

Obviously, I do not mean to suggest any change in the form of our present religious structures. I do not believe there can be any religion without loyalty and devotion to specific religious faiths and denominations. I do not know how God can be served except through the idioms and dialects of our various traditions. But the time has come to discover a means for fostering this institutional loyalty, and at the same time, an understanding of the common purposes and goals of all religion; to bring about unity and mutual appreciation and love among men of all religions, despite their differences and distinctions, and without any desire to minimize or compromise them.

In such an effort, I hope this very Fellowship of The Institute for Religious and Social Studies and our sister Fellowships in Chicago, and in Boston, may play a real part. Perhaps the ideas being forged here may become a means of winning men in far wider circles to the mutual understanding and affection which bring us together, and which we hope is a real contribution to world peace.

IX

FREEDOM AND INTERFERENCE IN AMERICAN EDUCATION

BY

ORDWAY TEAD

American education does not operate in a vacuum in either its administrative or educational phases. That there are freedoms to be preserved and interferences which should not supervene, is a truth worthy of thought more careful than is usually accorded to the tensions implicit in the situation. Indeed, in differing ways the situation presents difficulties today which merit explicit statement and study at every level of educational operation. If excuse be necessary, that is the reason for raising the questions which follow in this analysis.

How are loyalties of the numerous, special interest groups in our society to be expressed in relation to the overall control of education, so as to assure a defensible moral outcome in a larger public interest?

Assuming that education in action should be measurably "free," we have at once to ask—free for what, free from whom, free for whom? If we want to avoid interferences with educational processes which are selfish, uninformed, or undemocratic in intent, how are such interferences to be recognized, and by whom; and how are they to be confronted and any adverse influences to be offset?

With all this as the underlying problem before us, I shall try to make brief answer to the following more specific questions:

1. What is our educational system as a whole intended to do?
2. Is there wide agreement about this, and if not, what are the contemporary issues upon which people and groups differ and come into conflict?

3. To what kinds of agencies have we in America given the responsibility for resolving all such tensions of outlook and conviction?

4. What are some typical instances of contentious issues which have to be confronted in practice?

5. What are some of the underlying realities of our social psychology that make these conflicts difficult?

6. And, finally, are there some elements, factors, and programs of a remedial character which we can think through and apply as the occasion may require?

1. and 2. It might seem, superficially, that the problem of what American education is about, or is designed to do, would admit of the readiest of answers. And yet, when we come to scrutinize educational philosophy, educational practice, and educational leadership—because that is what it comes down to—we realize that up and down our land we face a condition more chaotic than we like to admit.

This problem can be variously stated. One way to put it is that there are those who think that education is designed primarily as a conserving influence on behalf of the intellectual and spiritual goods and values derived from the traditions of the past.

Next, there are those who think that education should be designed to interpret the present effectively for competent living.

And, there are those—and they are vehement protagonists, although in the minority—who think the purpose of education is the reformation of society.

Professor Edgar S. Brightman has somewhere made a suggestive statement about the relation of education to its culture, when he says that in any given society, education tends to stress one of three aims: to contemplate and participate in the eternal; to contemplate the past and present fact; or to contemplate the remaking of the future. My own view would be that education in its philosophy and practice should simultaneously hold all three in a rightful balance and interweaving of influence. Yet having said that, I might add that in general the influences or groups in society which would dwell on the past in education are usually most strong; those intent upon the present, somewhat less strong; and those who would emphasize the future typically the weakest of all.

Again, in relation to unity of educational objectives, it has in all honesty to be recognized that American school boards or school committees tend broadly to administer under certain preconceptions which affect the conduct of education—sometimes directly and sometimes only indirectly. I refer to the total standards of an Anglo-Saxon "middle class" tradition, of a so-called "free enterprise" system, of a society which has been shifting rapidly from being agricultural and small scale in economic operation to being urban and large scale.

Another way of stating the sharp differences of approach which occur among the "educationalists" themselves, is to use their own language and identify (1) the traditionalists or essentialists with "subject centered" instruction; (2) the progressives at the other pole who see the process as always "student centered" and as "reconstructionist" in purpose; and (3) the middle group who want individual growth in the current society looking to reciprocal, meliorative efforts, both upon individuals and within the structural arrangements of society.

Still a further opposition of view is that at the secondary and upper levels between a liberal arts and a vocational focus and emphasis. Both the vested interests of teachers and the preconceptions of citizens upon this issue are strong and not easily disturbed. Some would hold firmly to the liberal arts; some would strengthen vocational training for all; some would seek some combination and reconciling in one curriculum of both aims.

There is, furthermore, the confusion of purpose resulting when the cry is raised that our country is supplying "too much education for too many." This position has both honest and selfish protagonists. Those who hold to this view for whatever reasons do not always, however, take account of present realities as to the processes of selecting those who now attend college and the restrictions which exist to delay many qualified high school students from having the college opportunity which would further enhance their capacities and their usefulness. These protagonists seem to me to fail to face up to the numerous handicaps which are still to be met today by young people of superior ability desiring to secure a college education—handicaps which continue to deprive us of the trained capacities of many able youngsters. For the established fact is that obstacles which are economic, racial, geographic, of color, those of prior educational inequalities, all work today to debar thousands of well qualified boys and girls from going to college.[1] If the point is advanced that at the secondary level the instruction offered is not best suited to the majority of today's adolescents, that is a valid objection of a different kind, to be differently corrected.

Speaking in more administrative terms, we find a perennial source of profound tensions manifested recurrently in almost every local and state community—namely, to spend, or not to spend; to tax, or not to tax. Certain of our special interest groups appear to be typically on the side of budget retrenchment, irrespective of the merits of the claims for greater outlay; and such resistances naturally mean that all improvements have to be "sold" with the greatest possible persuasiveness to the majority of our citizens, if they are to be adopted in practice.

Finally, I mention a source of difference of view as between those who believe that all education has become far too "secularized"—by which is usually meant devoid of moral, ethical, and spiritual focus, interest, or motive—and those who are fearful that any changes on this score might bring organized religious influences more prominently into play. Feelings on this topic run high; but there remains the possibility that some kind of middle position can be arrived at which might be acceptable to both groups.

With this array of tensions about objectives, purposes, and methods, is it any wonder that issues about freedom and about interference arise and have to be faced?

3. In what areas, then, are decisions to be made as to the choices among divergent outlooks and genuine conflicts of policy—both sincere and selfish? In its present complexities, the problem has been recognized all too little; and the first task is to analyze its elements.

In general terms, the impetus to education in our country has had

[1] See for further documentation, *Higher Education for American Democracy*, The Report of the President's Commission for Higher Education, Harper & Brothers, New York, 1948, Part II.
Ordway Tead, *Equalizing Educational Opportunities Beyond the Secondary School*, Harvard University Press, Cambridge, 1947.

its grass roots in the local community. The local school committee or school board, democratically constituted by election or appointment, has been supervising and administering the foundation of our whole educational structure. Yet there are important diversities of operating method which can be suggested here.

There are those school boards all over the nation which are charged to raise their own budgets by special taxing powers granted to them. And there is the other type of school support, where the budget becomes a part of a general municipal budget, which the school board has to justify to the usual local budgetary authority.

A related problem, enhanced as urban populations have grown, is the actual effectiveness of school board operation—including the selection of able members, their grasp of educational processes, their integrity, and their overall wisdom in dealing with the professional educators.

We have, moreover, above the local boards, the increasing influence (interference here would seem to me too invidious a word) of state superintendents of schools or state boards of education or such a body as the Board of Regents in New York State. The diversity of provisions on this score from state to state is great. The range is from an annually elected, poorly paid, and poorly staffed "state superintendent" with ineffectual powers to level up local standards, a condition which prevails in some dozen states, up to the strong and ably administered state supervision exercised in New York State. In this state, supervision extends over the entire range of educational efforts, public and private, at every level, with the purpose of upholding standards of teacher selection, curriculum, library and building facilities, budgets, etc. That such oversight may on occasion be deemed by some to step over into interference, is not to be denied. But, broadly viewed, the need for a reasonably strong state supervisory agency seems to me to have been demonstrated. Nevertheless, in practice the individual educational system or institution will no doubt continue to experience a sense of what is at least annoyance and at worst a valid sense of grievance due to excessive efforts at the state level toward standardization. Demands for local freedom and for state interference with it are thus always potential sources of tension, just as state freedom and Federal interference might increasingly become a comparable source.

A still other kind of organized interposing in the conduct of education comes from our peculiar American method of legislating at the state level to require instruction in the schools on specified subjects. We have seen this dubious prerogative exercised in behalf of often worthy purposes; but that it is a sound method of guiding the development of curricular content, there are few educators who would agree with any enthusiasm. This kind of mandating has been undertaken in various states to assure the teaching of American history, safety, the consumer cooperative movement, and other special subjects. Indeed, there are further instances of certain legally required studies in the field of health and hygiene from which students from certain religious groups are exempted by law.[2]

A further organized provision which looks to the leveling up of the performance of secondary, higher, and professional education is the so-called voluntary accrediting agency. These bodies, cooperatively organized from representatives of the institutions of the region, seek by periodic surveys to hold member institutions to high standards of professional performance. At the graduate school level, the national professional association itself usually sets and regulates the standards. This device has been on the whole a salutary one; yet there is no denying that occasionally the degree and vigor of the "interference" (especially at the graduate school level) can be unwarranted, arbitrary, and too inflexible in a conservative direction. On the whole, however, the accreditation machinery over the years has within itself the means for the correction of its own excesses of undue interference.

Above the school board level, there are, moreover, in the college and university world, the boards of trustees of public and private institutions—sometimes politically appointed, sometimes elected; sometimes self-perpetuating, occasionally accorded life tenure. A volume called *Men Who Control Our Universities* [3] reminds us that there

[2] See C. E. Willgoose, *School and Society*, "Health, Welfare, Religious Freedom," March 31, 1951, p. 198.
[3] H. P. Beck, King's Crown Press, New York, 1947.

Freedom and Interference in American Education

may from time to time arise problems of interference with educational autonomy which have to be dealt with in the conduct of higher education. The typical trustee approach to the administrative problem tends to be that of business executives drawn from the larger corporations, whose patterns of managerial thinking tend to be transferred to deliberations on educational matters with not always the most wholesome results. It would surely be fatuous to deny that the hazard of trustee interference with educational affairs is one that may constitute a possible sporadic threat under present methods of trustee selection and operation.[4]

4. Although I may have thus far stressed the agencies that give voice to the tensions, they are all in varying degrees also responsible for helping to confront and resolve whatever conflicts may arise. Yet even before their role in this direction is thus suggested, it will be valuable to mention a few of the specific issues which are typically having to be met, in terms both of personal and of procedural reasons of conflict.

In local communities personal and business interests may all too readily color in limiting ways the views of individual school board members, whether because of real estate connections, religious views, or business interests of one kind or another.

There is also the possible threat of outside organizations moving into a city to discredit the work of professional educators and to seek to arouse local sentiment to effect their resignation. Ominous testimony of such incidents was offered at the convention of the American Association of School Administrators in Atlantic City early in 1951. Organized forces of reaction against the more modern influences in educational policy have thus become a new element in the picture of overall tensions; and they have already been instrumental in helping to force the removal of several able superintendents of schools.

Again, specific issues arise periodically as to the use of certain textbooks which have incurred the displeasure of some organized group, often a "patriotic" society with somewhat reactionary convictions. There have in recent years been too many instances where texts have

---

[4] See on the more constructive side, Ordway Tead, *Trustees, Teachers, Students: Their Role in Higher Education,* University of Utah Press, 1951.

been removed from use because, on grounds economic, social, or religious, some group or body finds a few sentences which offend its sensibilities.[5] In general, it may be said that such pressures have been as uninformed, prejudiced and retrogressive as they have been virulent and insistent.

We are familiar also with the interferences of those who believe that individual school principals or teachers are too "leftist" in their views. Testimony is far too general, for example, from high school teachers of "social science" courses that these have been watered down and thinned out, because of fears that the outspoken boldness of teachers would lead to reprisals of one kind or another. Nothing could be more ironic than to contemplate the introduction of courses designed to familiarize high school students with the contemporary social scene, only to have the exposition so tempered by timidity that a false and inadequate view is imparted.

At the college level, this problem can become more varied. Some teacher, for example, may circulate a questionnaire on sex matters for his girl students to answer, and upon the objection of some mother, his resignation is called for. Or another teacher makes a public utterance critical of the economic value of advertising, and some prominent alumnus demands that he be removed or at least silenced. Or a teacher announces to his class his disbelief in God, and church members and parents become aroused to call for his dismissal.

In all of this kind of attempted censorship, direct and indirect—and it can take many forms—my own opinion is that the pressures are not primarily those of wealth and money as such. They are usually the result of the outlooks of conventionally minded and loyal alumni or friends of the college, who honestly believe that the institution is being harmed because some professor has pronounced too extremely on some economic, religious, or other issue. And the predominant need is that the head of each college shall have sufficient courage, tact, and patience to resist such pressures in the interest of academic integrity.

Beyond this kind of interference, are the situations where there is

[5] See Sar A. Levitan, "Professional Organization of Teachers in Higher Education," *The Journal of Higher Education*, March, 1951, p. 123.

allegation of actual membership of some individual teachers in the Communist party, leading to trials and dismissals, which however justified and necessary, may tend to create fear and a sense of insecurity among other teachers who have no taint of such affiliation.

At the college level, also, recourse has been had to special loyalty oaths, and insistence upon these has been generally regarded by professors as an intrusion upon their freedom and an invidious interference with their professional integrity. Surely anyone familiar even to a slight extent with the tactics of the Communists, should realize that the requirement of a special oath will not identify those whom it is sought to identify or remove. On the other hand, every honest teacher feels his intellectual good faith is being impugned by such an extra oath being insisted upon solely from members of this profession. The use of special and extra teacher oaths is, in my opinion, a most unhappy and unacademic interference.

Again, we have found from time to time in certain state universities political interferences of a blatant sort, centering in the relation of the trustees to the state's political administration. Approaches to a corrective of such abuses are certainly easier to suggest than to have accepted in action!

Finally, on the score of potential interferences should be mentioned the possibilities of unwarranted Federal controls at whatever time Federal funds may be made more generally available for higher education in local areas. A vigorous statement of the dangers here is set forth by Professor John Diekhoff in his recent book, *Democracy's College*,[6] and such warnings will, of course, have to be heeded. Perhaps the most influential statement of the opposed view occurs in the Report of the President's Commission on Higher Education where the judgment is expressed (supported by other pronouncements from many prominent educators) that there can be adequate safeguards provided by local institutions to prevent unjustified Federal controls.

If the interference of Federal influences with the conduct of colleges and universities is to be realistically viewed, reference should be made to the possible influence of military thinking, as manifested in the conduct of ROTC's, and also to the controls exercised by Fed-

[6] Harper & Brothers, New York, 1950.

eral agencies when they enter into contracts for academic research work.

The institutions of higher learning can be disingenuous about fears of Federal control which might conceivably result from the acceptance of Federal funds. For while, on the one hand, they voice such fears, on the other hand, they seek contracts for subsidized Federal research or for branches of some form of officer training units on their campus, in both of which commitments the Federal controls are already known to be a fact.

Federal funds for higher education in the form of scholarships, outright grants, and capital loans, are probably imminent in the next few years; and in certain parts of the country they are already greatly needed. If, as this Federal participation in financial support is extended, it brings excessive interference with it, this will be due to carelessness and lack of thoughtful attention to the terms of new legislation and of the regulations under which it is carried out. I do not myself share the misgivings of those who believe this will be one more unfortunate curb upon the academic freedoms which need to be protected.

5. Before I conclude with a few suggestions of approaches to remedial measures, a few words are in order as to certain underlying social psychological realities in this problem, which inevitably qualify any programs for improvement.

(a) In the nature of the social dialectic of focusing now on freedom and now on some socially prompted interference in education, I think we should realize that quite properly the tensions here will be *perennial,* even though they may take ever differing forms of expression. In other words, efforts to interfere in ill advised ways will always be potentially present in a democratic society.

(b) The pressures upon educators for conformity to currently accepted standards and methods will always be profound. The burden of proof is always placed upon the educational innovator.

(c) For this reason the lag will be all too characteristic between professional knowledge about how best to carry on education, and our acceptance and support as citizens of the recommended programs.

(d) Fear and a sense of insecurity which retard desirable innovations by professional educators, are factors of increasing impact in periods of uncertainty such as we confront today.

(e) Efforts to counteract honest expressions of opinion, even when these are frankly anti-democratic, are hazardous if they lead to demands for repression of such utterances.

(f) We have the right to take heart and faith from a realization that the present size, complexity, and difficulty of the problem of universal public education in our land are newly come upon us. The recent, rapid growth in numbers of students alone presents a staggering problem. And we should never forget that no other nation has ever set out upon such an ambitiously inclusive program as ours is. We are properly required to temper our discouragements at all the shortcomings we acknowledge by possessing enough patience and persistence to hold us to the task.

(g) On the part of the whole educational fraternity, the one most valuable virtue in our day can be *courage*. This need extends from bottom to top and it entails courage to think independently upon social issues and to teach creatively with fresh methods. I understand why administrators and teachers are timid; I know their burdens and insecurities. And there must come a righting of many wrongs of commission and omission as to the status of the teacher in society. But when all else is said, the freedom of the educators from unwarranted interference requires as an indispensable condition their own *courage to act freely*.

(h) Similarly, there is no substitute for a developed and healthy sense of public responsibility on the part of our citizens. An informed local public opinion responsive to the registering of informed decisions—this is a basic key to the solution of problems of freedom and interference in the public schools. No legislation can be a substitute for a body of honest citizens who are sharing responsibility for oversight of the conduct of local education; and equally, unless the school board itself is composed of quality citizens, freedom from interferences will not be assured. Until enough people of integrity and devotion will serve on the trustee bodies of all educational agencies, most other corrective measures will mean little. Eternal and intelligent vigilance is the price of freedom from stupid or selfish interference.

In short, there are no easy answers here; but there are real, vital, and practical approaches to solutions.

6. In constructive terms, therefore, the following suggestions seem to me to bear closely upon the protective influences which should be generated for our assistance in these troubled areas.

Perhaps first in importance, it should be urged that in approaching present objectives and methods, there has to come a greater respect for the contemporary knowledge of the best professionals. Citizens who are still thinking in terms of "now when I went to school," have to realize that much valuable water has passed over the dam of educational methodology in thirty years. For we do know a great deal more than even twenty years ago about pedagogical techniques.

Second, we need a national, disinterested study about the wisest possible ways of selecting school boards and college boards of trustees. At the college level, for example, there are special problems to be faced, such as the desirable length of terms of trustees, their eligibility for reappointment, maximum age limits, the wisdom of their life tenure, etc.

Third, we need in local school systems and in college faculties better methods for assuring that relevant opinion, sentiment, and agreement to policy *flow up from the teacher*. If there is to be a minimum of undesirable interference, the professionals, in any system or institution, have to participate more fully in democratically shared deliberations, periodically assured, as to purposes, programs, and procedures.

Fourth, at the level of the overseeing agency, the school board of trustees, the lay members will usually profit by more direct, explicit, and continuing representation of the professional views of the educators themselves. In the not too distant future, selected teachers and principals will, I believe, be found in regular attendance along with superintendents, to clarify and strengthen the policy decisions of school boards. And a similar truth will some day apply to faculty representation on college trustee bodies. Such suggestions are in harmony with all we now know about the ways of enlisting and using to the full the creative power and productive initiative of those who are on the educational firing line. The release of the individual powers of teachers requires their sharing in determining the conditions under which the best professional achievement can take place. What I have elsewhere described in detail [7] as "the principle of the representation of interests," seems to me, in short, in need of being invoked in appropriate ways in educational policy making bodies.

Fifth, we will not get the fullest values out of the interrelations of local and state educational bodies until state boards of education in most states are strengthened in staff, budget, and powers of oversight. This is obviously a step each state will have to take within its own borders. And much can be learned from the experience of the great state of New York, both as to what to do and what not to do in amplifying the role of a state board in other states.

Sixth, everything possible should be done by administrators, boards, and citizens' groups to protect the freedom of utterance of teachers. The truth seeking, truth teaching aspects of the teachers' role are uniquely valuable and should be valiantly defended up to the point where subversive doctrines are being dispensed by the teacher, which activity becomes a clear breach of public trust.

Seventh, a weakness which is in great need of study and correction is: how to keep the general public informed and convinced in a contemporary way as to the needs and the desirable programs of the professional educators. There is, in my opinion, a lag between pedagogical knowledge and educational performance in the school systems up and down the land of from twenty to twenty-five years. Many citizens are still misunderstanding and resisting as "frills and fads" the pedagogical fundamentals and their applications which two decades ago were proved to be worthy. The task of interpreting by intensive public relations efforts what education ought to be, to do, and to cost, is one the professional educators have slighted to the immense weakening of good educational performance. For the fact is, I repeat, that we know far more than we practice in the conduct of education.

In conclusion, these several suggestions should, if intelligently ap-

[7] See my *Democratic Administration,* Association Press, New York, 1945, Part I.

plied, help to preserve the needful educational freedoms and to ward off the most inept interferences. And all this will be of immeasurable value, because unwholesome pressures are now too many and too stultifying in their effects.

I repeat, however, that in one sense this problem will *never* be wholly resolved. Nor should this surprise or disappoint us, assuming that it may increasingly be assured that so long as all the influences of interference are identified and in the open.

But the professional educator will, for example, keep on coming up with new methods and techniques. And adults, including responsible trustees, will continue to be nostalgic about the good old days and ways.

Eager and conscientious teachers, to offer another example, will happily continue to be vocal as to opinions and convictions with which some groups in the community may not agree and will seek to silence.

The approach to a temporary resolution of such inevitable tensions has already been suggested. The diverse groups in our society should have every encouragement, in short, to "speak their piece" before the appropriate deliberative body. The groups directly interested in education should be brought together on a democratic, representative basis where policy forming and oversight are going forward. A greater sharing by the closely affected groups in decision making promises to assure fuller guarantees of rightful freedoms, and a protection against unwise interferences.

And continuingly the obligation is upon all who are informed about the better educational ways and means, to be articulate and persuasive in interpreting to a wide public the wisdom of making use of enlightened programs and of supporting them with adequate financial resources. Such assuring of strong support with its wide base of public acceptance becomes itself the single greatest guarantee that education will remain free to fulfil its rightful mission. For this will mean that an informed opinion in each institutional unit is always standing ready to protect and advance an enlightened public interest to offset any one which may be limited and self-seeking.

X

PRIVATE PROFIT AND PUBLIC INTEREST IN MASS COMMUNICATION

BY

ROBERT SAUDEK

I come before you as the prodigal son returned, momentarily, to the society of learned men. Outside that door you will find a uniformed ABC page boy resting on a butterfly net. After one hour he will take me back to Radio City in my camisole. Do not sympathize. I shall feel more comfortable. For I have noted that of all the thirteen speakers who are addressing this group on "Morals and Loyalties"—five are called professor, four doctor, a dean, and a president—I am the only one who could reply to the naked question, "What is your title?" by whispering, "Call me Mister."

You have read the subject assigned to me. George Bernard Shaw undertook, in his play called *Major Barbara,* to discuss another conflict between private profit and public interest. His dealt with the field of charity. I have heard the wives of university presidents lament on this same conflict as it frustrated their husbands' unsuccessful efforts to raise funds for an economics fellowship while riding at anchor on a well heeled alumnus' steam yacht off Bar Harbor. Conflicts of this nature may be found in education, welfare work, politics, radio, television, the newspapers and, in fact, in religion. I read with special interest in *Time* magazine recently of a long forgotten classmate of mine, minister in a church in Alton, Illinois, whose concern for tolerance in his church and in his community lost him the financial and then even the spiritual support of his parishioners. He was asked to resign—and I suppose the congregation added—without prejudice.

I do not come here as a professional apologist for the mass media, radio, newspapers, television, and magazines. Nor would I beat my breast and confess their sins. I have spent some years in the commercial aspects of radio, and I devote a major part of my time now to the public interest phases of radio and television.

This is what I have learned: that the mass media are not unlike the class media; that the mass media are not unlike the people who produce them, or the people for whom they are produced. I am not competent to say what it is that makes men and women devote a portion of their energies to philanthropy, or to P.T.A. activities, or to church going, or to the Boy Scouts, or to the election of lawmakers who are pledged to deal promptly with child labor, wage and hour standards, low rental housing, workmen's compensation, freedom of worship, personal liberty, and independent courts of justice.

A quarter century ago it was fashionable to say that economics was the foundation upon which our moral history is built. This was the Gospel according to Frederick Jackson Turner, and a tarnished gospel it was.

In more recent times the moral, the thoughtful, and the unselfish acts of man have been attributed by psychiatry to man's guilt feelings. These are but compensatory impulses, say many psychiatrists, for all the evil we think we have done. And they hasten to assure us that evil is a fictitious concept made up of the inhibitions of the bourgeois morality, including many things from premature toilet training to sibling rivalry, suppressed aggression, and Momism.

A third school would hold, with Machiavelli, that the ego and self-esteem are best served by calculating one's gifts. Christmastime is the time to buy affection from your family, your neighbors, and your employees. It is the time to tip the county clerk, and then ask for your initials on your license plates. It interprets a gift to be a bribe.

And to these that sterling example of modern literature now holding its place in the firmament of best sellers, Hauser's *Look Younger, Live Longer*. This would put a moral value on parsley.

No scientist has yet been able to prove or disprove, by independent evidence, any one of these theories, because man responds to such a wide variety of stimuli, in so many ways, for such varying lengths of time, that even the International Business Machines Company

Private Profit and Public Interest in Communication

would be staggered at the idea of sorting out the conflicts at work in men's personalities.

It is apparent, however, that the conflict which we are here attempting to identify in the special field of the mass media is at work in nearly every field of human endeavor, not excepting that of religion. I am called upon almost weekly to act as a kind of unfrocked referee in many a churchly dispute involving the matter, for instance, of soliciting funds over the air; and there are cynics who tell me that one or another denomination—often among the so-called "splinter sects" —makes quite a tidy thing of its "publishing houses" and the like.

So we may do well to spend a moment considering the root of this conflict, of which its manifestation in mass media is one symptom.

The only political certainty in a democracy is the certainty that the rules we live by will reflect the mutations which we, as living, changing organisms, may undergo. What therefore appears to be an unstable quality of democracy has, in fact, a resilience, an elasticity which not only *withstands* a very pronounced buffeting about, but in fact thrives and grows on all the spirited exercise it gets. Compared with a monolithic society, the latter's apparent strength, built in as a rigid resistance to change, contains the seeds of its own weakness. To be specific, private profit and the public interest could not live side by side in such a society. The tensile strength would be so strained in a totalitarian government that one or the other must break.

No one has ever seriously proposed that democratic society is or ever will be devoid of conflicts. But it may be fairly stated that a democratic society gambles on the recurrence of the victories of its own better nature. Otherwise, one of two things would have occurred in the history of our own country: either it would have been so stagnant a history that we should now find ourselves governed by freeholders only, with private schools only, with male voters and male jurors only, with Negro slavery, and with none of the benefits of a long line of legislative and judicial actions promoting the general welfare and protecting the basic freedom and dignity of individual human beings—either it would be that stagnant, or the course of our nation's history would present an unbroken story of sordid retrogression, whereby the crimes against men's souls and bodies would have increased with the years, the wicked would go unpunished, and the good would go unrewarded.

So our father's house has many mansions. Our nation has many kinds of people. And those people, individually and in their relationships with one another, have many passions: we are neither sheep nor goats. The chemistries of our several personalities contain, among other things, jealousy, generosity, courtesy, ambition, appreciation, hatred, shyness, lust, chicanery, godliness, and a strong sense of brotherhood. Excepting for certain excessive symptoms, not one of these motivations of man is legislated against in the democracy. There is a wide tolerance allowed for the interplay of men's emotions.

Take the characteristic of slyness: there is an unpleasant sound to the word. Yet slyness has often caught a thief. Take the quality of ambition: men deny it in themselves, yet it has carried strong men to the seat of government, and it has made humble boys into great scientists.

All of this is a long way round to the particular topic of this paper. From time to time men of goodwill have seriously proposed that the conflict between private profit and the public interest, in newspapers, magazines, radio, or television, be resolved by legislating private profit out of existence in these media. There is no guarantee that this will actually solve the conflict; nor, more important, that it will not give rise, like dragon seeds, to a pair of new conflicts. But there is some history on the side of tolerating the conflict.

First, there is the history of improvement. It is perfectly conceivable, taking the newspapers as an example, that the medium of the printed page of information might have spread across the country without benefit of private ownership, and that people would today have a press free of the temptations which advertising puts in the path of some publishers. Also, it is possible that the size of the paper would not bear so direct a relationship to the amount of advertising sold in any edition. With enlightened government, the physical sources of the news, and its means of distribution might be as elaborate under public ownership as it is under private ownership.

But men, in or out of government, are made up of the same conflicting forces. The paper stock and the ink would be public property,

Private Profit and Public Interest in Communication

but the selection of words and ideas and arguments would be the private property of human beings who held official office.

How, then, could there have been an exposition of the Tea Pot Dome scandal? The men whose nefarious practices were exposed were the very men who would have manipulated public attitudes, lulled them to sleep, made them feel secure and trusting.

How, without private citizens at the printing press, would the City of New York have been aroused to turn out the Tweed Ring and Richard Croker?

In a less melodramatic framework, how would our people be able to shop in the marketplace of conflicting opinions; and how otherwise could the people, by exercising the franchise of free selection, encourage the editor who writes more plainly, who affords his paper more graphic pictures, who can provide a wider variety of more expensive commentators?

This seems strangely like a belated defense of the freedom of the press. I do not mean to come to you 170 years too late, wearing the disguise of the marked down Federalist. But it would appear that a large part of the matter at issue today relates to the tolerance which this nation has for the independent actions of its citizens, so long as they do not contravene the law.

To return to individuals once more, it may be fairly stated that there is a conflict in most of us which compels us to devote a substantial portion of our personal lives to private profit, at the expense of the public interest. For it is generally for private profit that we afford ourselves the smaller luxuries of life. I heard of a speaker in a nearby community who recently excoriated his audience of parents because they had not afforded their children a bicycle stand in front of their school. And he said to them, "If you had devoted the money you spent for cocktails today to a bicycle stand, you would have solved your problem."

Here was a conflict. Yet that speaker, whether or not he buys cocktails himself, drove to the auditorium in a Buick, although a Chevrolet would have taken him there as quickly, with $1000 left over to give to his church or his favorite charity. He resolved that personal conflict in favor of himself. But he also guided a group of parents to one possible solution favorable to the public welfare. No one of us can fairly claim that our own way of living is free of these personal conflicts; and few of us would solve our own conflicts in any way other than by tending generally in the right direction. Build a log cabin and whose birthplace have you built? Abraham Lincoln's, or Jesse James's? Build a mansion, and whose birthplace have you built? Benedict Arnold's, or George Washington's? The choice is not in the amount of your assets. It is in your way of using them.

We in the relatively new fields of the electronic media are distinguishable from our older brethren in the fact that we have a real and legal responsibility to serve the public interest. We meet our duty with varying degrees of success. But our assets and our solvency as licensees are likewise of mandatory concern to the licensing body. In writing the radio law, the Congress deliberately established a relationship between a broadcaster's financial condition and his ability to serve the public interest. Thus, financial stability is one measure of good faith; and in the expensive age of television it is nearly impossible to meet this requirement without passing the hat among those who have money to spend. So you have stockholders. Now, the nature of stock company laws is such that a corporation's management is obliged to use its best efforts to operate the company so as to realize some profit for the stockholders. And the nature of a broadcasting license is such that the licensee must operate in the public interest.

Is this such a serious conflict? Only the results can tell; and each man must decide by his own criteria whether the conflict is so sharp that private profit just is not compatible with public service.

Compulsion, in the United States, is an ugly word, yet its ugliness is sometimes lost, because it slides so conveniently off the tongue. Let me take you down through some of the places we have visited in this discussion, and show you how compulsion would look in place of conflict.

You compel the radio and television media to operate without profit; so the nation is poorer; for competitive networks and stations in any quantity would be wasteful of taxpayers' money. Then, for the remaining stations, you compel the uniformity of administration, of minds at work, of policies, of orchestras, of news reports. Economy would dictate part of this, and bigotry the rest.

You would compel newspapers to consolidate, simplify, standardize. You would compel magazines to conform, and you would choke off the ambition to create the full blown picture magazine, the highly competitive fiction and news magazines. You would create a single employer for magazine writers, and thus a price fixing monopoly to buy their stories.

Then you would go on and compel men to drive *volkswagons,* cheap, economical to operate, monotone in color, and with marginal comfort.

You would compel men to forego cocktails—or Coca-Colas, if you prefer—and to devote their savings to church causes.

But in the name of expediency and peace of mind there would be little reason to permit the conflicts that exist among religious faiths and denominations, so you would again resolve the conflict by establishing one church, compulsorily.

But hold on—there is a conflict between those in the top stories of apartment dwellings and those below. Compel them to rotate each year, and solve that conflict.

Then, as all criticism is born of conflict, eliminate criticism. Let the people vote, "*Ja.*"

Now, you have the perfect state. To cite your own title for this series, you will have imposed inflexible standards of both morals and loyalties. You have ended all conflict. What have you left? Compulsion. Compulsion by whom? Certainly not by you, for you could never agree on what to compel people to agree about. But I have brought you a solution for that, too. Because the world is full of men who would like the opportunity to impose compulsion in place of conflict. Find one of those men, and you will live happily ever after.

XI

THE THREAT TO PRIVACY

BY

HAROLD D. LASSWELL

Those of us who share the tradition of respect for human dignity, also participate in the tradition, that human dignity includes respect for privacy. In this paper I want to draw your attention to the peril in which this traditional respect for privacy stands in the modern world and to ask whether we should abandon the demand or whether, on the contrary, we should seek to save as much as possible from what is perhaps a sinking ship. My own mind is not wholly made up on many of the issues which I will pose.

Respect for privacy is threatened by the rapid increase of scientific and technical knowledge about how it can be encroached upon, and also by the intensity with which certain demands to invade privacy are propagated. I shall suggest that recent trends in modern civilization have been toward the restriction of privacy, and that these trends are likely to gain, rather than to lose, in the years ahead.

The Anglo-American trend contains rather considerable degrees of emphasis upon mutual regard for the privacy of the other individual. This is expressed in many conventional codes of conduct and especially in the legal arrangements by which the private individual is sought to be protected from encroachments on the part of officials, or of other private individuals. In our culture we are accustomed to abide by a number of informal conventions that circumscribe the degree to which it is permissible under various conditions to penetrate the other fellow's zone of privacy. We learn to live up to certain conventional reticences in dealing with strangers, casual acquaintances, friends and intimates. The scale of intimacy is itself connected with the permissive penetration of the walls which are maintained against the casual disclosure of thoughts, feelings—and deeds.

It would be a very rewarding enterprise to describe the topography of the American ego in reference to other egos as established by observant social and psychological scientists who have familiarized themselves with the United States. European observers, at least, have been impressed by the "open ego" that flourishes in this country. When they say this they have in mind the answers which are sometimes given to the question, "How many friends do you have?" Young people often lay claim to hundreds of friends. This is startling to those who have been brought up in cultures where the idea of a friend is highly circumscribed, and even calls for special ceremonies to inaugurate the intimate forms of address (such as the German, "*du*"). More careful statements on the matter emphasize the formidable differences which prevail within the same culture, according to the social class of the individual. It is generally believed among us that lower class persons (measured in terms of respect or wealth position) lay much less store by the demand for privacy than the upper or middle class person.

Furthermore, there are occupational (skill) differences that modify the picture, even for individuals whose wealth or respect position is the same. It is often said, for instance, that invasions of privacy are much more prevalent and less noticed among actors than among scholars.

The truth of the matter is that we are very imperfectly informed about the zones of privacy which are expected to be adhered to in the various situations comprised in Western European culture as a whole or our own variant thereof. Nor, as I shall suggest a little later on, are we too well informed about the trends in these patterns. I know that some physicians, nurses, psychologists, and social workers say that middle and upper class Americans are more secretive about their financial position than about the details of their sex lives. But whether this, if a valid observation, marks a new trend or the continuation of the old one, I do not know.

When we examine the body of legal doctrines and observances

relating to privacy, we are on surer ground than when we try to describe the zones of informal privacy. The formal arrangements are matters of public record and are well known to the legal profession.

Let me remind you of some of the restrictions which have been affirmed, at least until the recent past, upon the government official in England and the United States. We forbid officials to invade the privacy of the individual unless specific authority has been granted by a court. This is thought of as defending the home and the workplace from arbitrary search and seizure of records and other objects.

We forbid police agents to conceal their identity from individuals and to induce their unwitting victims to commit an offense. This limitation arose in part from the experience that crime may be increased by the zeal of police agents to entrap victims. Blackmail, too, is presumably fostered by entrapment.

We put the burden of finding proof of an alleged criminal act upon the public official. Hence, we forbid the use of coercive methods, in order to compel a confession from the accused. This restriction arises in part from the experience that the confessions resulting from a coercive violation of privacy are often false. We also allow the accused to refuse to answer on the ground that the answer might incriminate him. If an individual is charged with a crime or arrested, he is to have notice of the fact that his admission may be used against him. Experience shows that innocent persons may make self-accusing statements, for such reasons as the desire to shield a beloved person or as a result of blackmail.

We have statutes of limitations which exempt the individual from answering for many faults which he has committed in the distant past. One function of such statutes is to protect the privacy of individuals from malevolent prying. The practice also enables human beings to wipe the slate clean and start over again, free of the opprobrium which is attached to criminal proceedings.

In civil litigation (that is, a dispute involving only private parties) the defendant receives a great deal of protection in his privacy, although by no means as complete as in the case of the defendant against criminal accusations. One is protected, of course, against searches and seizure without a warrant from a court. The defendant is not to be coerced by a private individual who tries to extract admissions from him. The ordinary rules of litigation provide no little protection against invasions of privacy. For example, the rules of evidence are supposed to prevent the dragging into the open of information which is not germane to the issue, and whose only function is to stigmatize the individual in the eyes of judge and jury.

The rules also prevent the violation of confidences. The confessional relationship is usually respected, as are the relations of physician and patient or lawyer and client. Although the rules do not say so, a professional newspaperman is usually exempt from disclosing his sources of information.

Some protection of privacy is given as an incident to the rule which requires the corroboration of statements alleged to have been overheard or received in a private talk. Partial protection is given to third parties against disparagement in public.

It is also customary to conduct some litigation in private; notably divorce cases, proceedings that involve minors, testimony which is deemed shocking to the mores or deleterious to public decency. Many stages of criminal complaint and investigation are kept secret, with the result that some unfounded allegations, at least, are not widely disseminated.

Whether by statute or administrative practice, many official agencies refrain from disclosing information about individuals which is usually regarded as within the domain of privacy. The Census, for example, does not divulge information about specific individuals, nor does the Treasury. The Social Security Administration is another agency that has many intimate details on file. So, too, do public hospitals, the Selective Service System, and the like.

Criminal sanctions are both threatened and applied against public officials or private individuals who transgress many of the limits within which the individual may operate on his own. Criminal codes usually proscribe and penalize such actions as obtaining money from someone on threat of disclosing information which will damage his reputation.

So much for a few of the official and unofficial patterns of respect for privacy. What concerns us especially is that the expansion of modern science and invention has developed a host of means by which it is possible to penetrate the traditional zones. With the telephone came the "telephone tap," which made it feasible to "listen in" on other people's conversations. When the microphone was developed, concealed microphones could be placed in any room in any building. With the modern camera, all sorts of new possibilities were realizable. Ultra-red photography enables a record to be made without a flash bulb. The distance lens adapts itself to the needs of a "peeping tom" at very long range, or in unconventional locations, for observing what goes on in neighboring apartments or office buildings. One-way glass makes it feasible to watch the conduct of persons who imagine they are wholly unobserved.

Many physiological instruments have been adapted to so-called "lie detection" purposes. One of the commonest devices provides a tracing of the action of the heart, registered in the form of a record of the pulse. It is also possible to make a continuous tracing of variations in the conductance by the skin of an electrical current of known strength. A continuous tracing can be taken of an expanding and contracting chest in the act of breathing.

Perhaps the most startling results are those which are obtained by the use of drugs or hypnosis, singly or in combination. Subjects can be induced to reveal their entire life history even to the most intimate details of early life. Moreover, these procedures can be applied in such a way that the subject has no recollection that he has made a disclosure.

I do not want to create an exaggerated impression of what can be accomplished by the methods at present available. A degree of voluntary cooperation is essential to the success of some of these procedures. A recalcitrant subject can defeat the ordinary lie detection methods. Even willing subjects do not always respond fully, when they are hypnotized or in a state of hypnosis. But practical experience has shown that voluntary cooperation on the part of the subject is by no means always essential. Many subjects imagine they can "beat the machine," but fail to control involuntary responses that tell the investigator what he wants to find out. Also it is possible to get results in an unknown percentage of cases by dazing the subject with a tap on the head or by means of drugs administered covertly in the food or drink. Initial resistance can be worn down by methods which have been described in connection with procedures of the police of totalitarian states.

Imperfect as existing methods are, they clearly indicate that the time is not far distant when all private thoughts, feelings, and reminiscences are vulnerable to methods of enforced disclosure. This means that from a scientific and technical point of view, privacy will be a thing of the past, in the sense that secrets of living people can be obtained at will. Actually we are not far from that day. We have the techno-scientific means of abolishing respect for privacy.

Side by side with this trend toward solving the purely technical problems involved, another trend can be discerned. This is the growth of demands to use the new devices for the penetration of hitherto inaccessible areas of human life. Some of these initiatives come from persons who are skilled in the use of the new instruments, and who are absorbed in the purely technical task of carrying a method to the highest degree of refinement. Often they are entirely oblivious to the significance of what they are doing for the conception of respect for privacy. The idea has never crossed their minds.

A good illustration is the candid camera and the application of the new devices evolved in modern photography. The pioneers in "snapping" people under all circumstances do not think of themselves as the vanguard of contempt for human dignity. On the contrary, in so far as such ideological issues rise to the level of awareness, the candid camera movement is thought of in quite moralistic terms. Many camera addicts believe they are familiarizing everyone with the facts of how everybody else looks (and hence providing some clue to how they think, feel, and operate). They think they are providing permanent historical documentation of life in our time.

A wounded man writhing in agony on the street after a traffic accident, a mother's face transfixed with horror as her child drops from a building, a dowager baring a shank at the opera, a President having trouble with a strand of spaghetti, a sailor and a girl necking on a park bench—all are assumed to be legitimate material for public recordation. (The "right" of the individual to control photographs made of him has not even been fought out in the courts.)

Of course, the media of mass communications are the ones which have taken the most active interest in dissolving old barriers. They allowed their cameramen and reporters to go into the sensational details of murder, rape, divorce, and the like, guided solely by the opportunities for "circulation building." Anybody who challenges these practices is likely to be assailed as an enemy of "freedom of the press." The publishers claim special immunities even when they have no standards to apply, save the market standards of all businesses.

However, some of the most farreaching invasions of privacy come from policymakers who desire to cut down their risks by making use of the knowledge which has become available, or which can become available, by the procedures developed by psychologists and social scientists for therapeutic or purely scientific purposes. In a large organization an ever present problem is in the selection and promotion of personnel. Everyone admits that the decline and fall of many corporations in the business world is connected with mistaken judgment in the choice of top and middle management. It is also understood that the costs of production are affected by the lack of gratification experienced by the rank and file employees on the job. Hence there has been an expanding concern on the part of modern management for the selection of workers on the basis of tests of aptitude for the performance of various tasks. In recent times there is an increasing stress on congeniality, and hence upon temperament tests. The modern management is impressed by the results of sociological studies of the small group, and the ways in which congenial relationships can be established and maintained. The demand for more intimate knowledge of persons eligible to be top executives, has led to the encouragement of psychiatric and other appraisals. Although the details are kept in medical or technical confidence, the frequency, and depth, and exhaustiveness of the penetration into privacy are striking.

The most striking concentration of incentives making for disclosure occur, of course in the realm of national security. By this time Americans are adjusting themselves to the continuing crisis of insecurity in world affairs. I do not need to dilate upon the continuing threat of war as the world moves toward power bipolarity (the United States *versus* the Soviet bloc). Even if there is no World War III, the perpetual crisis is likely to bring grave transformations in our way of life, and especially in our willingness to protect individual freedom. As the garrison-prison state pattern is more closely approximated, invasions of privacy are to be anticipated. In this country already we have seen large scale invasions of privacy which have been justified in the name of national security. We all have in mind the loyalty program which subjected all federal employees to police investigation. It is possible that police inquiries of this kind will become more, rather than less, characteristic of American life, as the crisis continues and even intensifies. Before private business concerns can receive many types of defense contracts, they must be scrutinized as potential security risks. The workers in many defense plants are already subject to investigation. Universities are applying for contracts from the government for research and teaching programs, many of which depend upon security clearances of administrators, faculty, and students.

It is hardly necessary to say that under these circumstances the burden of surveillance that is put upon the agencies which perform the political police function is exceedingly heavy. Manpower is always in somewhat short supply during a period of rapid expansion of any given function, and this provides a strong inducement to the taking of shortcuts. Police departments are already accustomed to gather information which they cannot present to the courts because of the methods used. Our courts, have been very reluctant to admit the results of a "lie detection" procedure as evidence. Yet in many places it is ordinary police routine to employ one of the standard methods of sifting suspects. This is usually justified on the ground of efficiency in clearing the innocent, and in exposing the most eligible suspects for further investigation. It is also maintained that "lie detection" reduces the use of third degree methods of physical brutality.

Courts have also been reluctant to admit as evidence information obtained by wiretapping or concealed microphones. But police departments have long made use of such methods, chiefly as a means of discovering suspects, and obtaining "leads" for the gathering of in-

The Threat to Privacy

formation by more acceptable procedures. Private detective agencies (of which there are several thousand in the United States) employ wiretapping and concealed microphones as regular routine. In the investigation of insurance claims, for example, this is one of the quickest ways of discovering whether injuries have been grossly exaggerated. And the number of spouses who have private detectives examining one another's conduct is not small.

Given this rising volume of police practice and the gradual acquiescence of courts in "shortcut" methods, it is reasonable to forecast that police invasions of privacy are likely to gain, rather than to lose, momentum during a continuing crisis of national insecurity.

It is commonly said (and I do not have the data for challenging this interpretation) that until rather recently the trend of historical development in Western countries was toward greater rather than less respect for individual privacy. If we look over the history of Anglo-American law, this seems to be well substantiated. It is probable that the demand for privacy became one of the distinguishing marks of individuals who occupied the most exalted position in Medieval England, for example, and that the demand gained definiteness and formal sanction in the course of the long struggle over the power of the monarchy. Certainly the traditional rights of Englishmen are crystallized in the conflict between the nobility and the crown. Evidently the sharing of power in English society carried with it a sharing of respect, which included some considerable respect for privacy. As the participants in power increased (upper nobility, lesser nobility, commoners who owned property, and so on) the informal and formal standards of the top elite were taken over by the ever more numerous members of the politically active classes.

In the United States our historians have made us conscious of the importance of horizontal mobility for the spread of respect (interpreted as privacy). By horizontal mobility is meant the movement of the people in space. It is a well known story how the spread of the population across the continent contributed to the sharing of respect, power, wealth, and other social values. Even if we qualify somewhat the famous hypothesis about the influence of the frontier on American development, enough remains to support the statement that men could get a new and relatively anonymous start in the areas successively called the West. Individuals and small groups did succeed in removing themselves from communities in which they were well known and going to places where they were comparative strangers. Hence they were able to suppress much of the past from the knowledge of the neighbors and business associates. It was often bad form to pry into the past, often for the reason there was something which the individual wanted to conceal.

Can we say that the weight of the factors making for privacy has changed in recent decades, and that the trend of historical development in America has for some time past been in the direction of restricting (and perhaps abolishing) privacy?

Consider first the significance of the factors connected with power which in the past appear to have cut an important figure in bringing about respect for privacy. It is probable that the intensity of concern for the sharing of power inside the nation has declined. This is not because the demand for democracy has been given up in despair, but because of the seeming triumph of universal suffrage and of other institutions through which the sharing of power is conventionally expressed. True, enough, important elements of the population are not fully included. But this is generally regarded as an exception, and one which is actually in the process of being abolished.

As intense concern for the sharing of power within the nation has diminished, other problems have gained in importance. Often the new problems have made for the removal of privacy. Consider, for example, the emergence of "crime" as a national issue. As our institutions become more complicated we call more offenses "crimes," and we have become aware of the dangers from organized crime. Offenders have often been members of the community with little or no moral standing among their fellows. I have in mind the thugs who flourished under Prohibition, and the gangs who engage in prostitution, gambling, drugs, and other "rackets." I suspect there has been an undertone of cumulative resentment against the corrupt politician and the flourishing criminal gangster. The impression has gained ground that our laws for the protection of the individual have too often been exploited for purposes of which we do not approve. Hence there is some "softness" toward practices on the part of private detectives, police, and courts, that contravene some of the traditional methods of protecting privacy.

In recent times the threat to democracy has seemed to lie outside the country. Fascists, Nazis, and Communists are all conceived as "foreign" menaces to our way of life. As the world is more sharply polarized and militarized, and the subversive American is more and more feared, I suspect that Americans are willing to take more risks connected with invasions of privacy, in order to get better protection against friends and agents of foreign enemies.

If the demand for privacy is no longer so actively sustained by an intense demand to share power inside the community, we may inquire whether the other big factor (horizontal mobility) continues to operate on behalf of privacy. The answer to this, I think, is evident. With the settlement of the continent and the enormous expansion of modern means of transportation and communication, people are no longer able to escape from their pasts by buying tickets. What is happening on a huge scale is the transformation of the United States (and indeed of the accessible globe) into a vast village. Horizontal mobility signified a sharp restriction in the intensity of direct human contact. With settlement and with the expansion of instruments of contact, lost intensities are being reestablished. Obviously, the restoration is being achieved on a scale never before considered possible.

Let me remind you of some of the operations of the "extended village." You may recall that after World War I the returning soldiers were something of a problem, even in victorious countries. In the United States there were many examples of disorganized conduct on the part of veterans who came back to the college campus. World War II has been remarkably without an aftermath of this kind. It is reasonable to attribute the rapid reassimilation of the American soldier in part to the fact that he never had a chance to get away from home. In World War I it took weeks for a letter to travel from Middletown to France and for the reply to come back. World War II introduced V-mail, which reduced the circuit time to a few days. Radio broadcasting and film kept the soldiers acquainted with the noise, as well as the sights, of the home land. With certain exceptions, notably in the Pacific, the intensity of contact between soldier and home folks was such that alienation and disorganization were sharply reduced.

I have not yet called attention to another important factor in reference to privacy, namely, that privacy has by no means been felt to be an unmitigated advantage. On the contrary, privacy has often been experienced as more deprivational than indulgent. One of the most characteristic complaints in modern civilization has been against the "impersonality" of modern industry and the destruction of warm personal relations.

In this connection we note that modern social science discovered the problem of "anomie," to employ Durkheim's successful term. Durkheim was impressed by the conspicuousness of suicide in modern nations and undertook to account for the prevalence of self-destruction. After scrutinizing basic trends and conditioning factors, he was eventually led to the conception of anomie, or lack of identification on the part of the primary ego of the individual with a "self" that includes others. In a word, modern man appeared to be suffering from psychic isolation. He felt alone, cut off, unwanted, unloved, unvalued. Even the image of the personal God appeared to recede, if not indeed to vanish, under the stare of accumulating scientific knowledge. The redefining of the image of God imposes a severe burden upon the common man.

The conception of anomie has been greatly enriched by the findings of modern clinical psychology. In the world of accelerating change, millions of persons are thrown into novel situations in both the ideological and operational sense. It is no longer possible to rely upon the automatic appropriateness of older ways of thinking and doing. Men and women must cope with uncertainty, and uncertainty is a fertile breeder of anxiety.

To the tensions of non-identification, we must add the tensions of choice, to which Erich Fromm has given such persuasive statements. The act of choice brings with it acute awareness of the ego as a distinct entity poised, as it were, with one foot in the air, trying to figure out where to step as the escalator of the future comes into view. The necessity of taking thought carries with it a sort of isolation, a sense of separation from the flow of familiar happenings. This is the privacy of thought which is so exhilarating to many gifted minds, and so agonizing to less "cerebral" types.

Intimately bound up with the tensions of which we have been speaking is the stress and strain of ambition. In our prodigious age, science and technology are opening new vistas of opportunity with every passing day. Expectations of success have intensified the competitive drives that set one individual apart from another. During the past century, for example, we saw the rapid expansion of competitive markets and competitive politics. Even the family institution came to depend less on older conceptions of propriety and more on the competitive lure of personal charm and whim. The individual psyche experienced the new opportunities, and translated them into strenuous demands for achievement. Actually the tensions of ambition have long been known to daily life and literature. It is known that ambition implies that all human relationships are viewed as instruments of further success. All human relations become "contacts," social intercourse is progressively subordinated to the end of social "climbing," or to the accumulation of wealth or power. Hence a demand for personal achievement is a strenuous "demand by self upon self, and others." And the ambitious man is an aloof man, no matter how many "contacts" he has every twenty-four hours in the dizzy grind of office, lunch, cocktails, dinner, and entertainment. When other persons are conceived, in opposition to the Kantian dictum, as means rather than ends in themselves, an act of withdrawal has occurred. The thinking and feeling ego transforms other human beings into manipulatable dummies who are to be "sold" a bill of goods, or a candidate, or some other "line." Hence the ego ends by depriving the surrounding world of its humanity, and, as a result, suffers from the dehumanizing effects of "splendid isolation" in a globe that has been demoted to a congregation of puppets. The ego gets farther and farther away from spontaneous human association, as he withdraws into the castle of the primary self.

I suspect that we are justified in saying that animosity against privacy is one of the major drives of our time and that this aversion to privacy arises from the deprivations which individuals have undergone as a byproduct of the tensions of non-identification, of choice, and of ambition.

If this interpretation is correct, we are dealing with a profound reversal of direction in the social institutions deemed appropriate to human dignity. It is more imperative than it has been for a long time that we reconsider the importance that we should attach to respect for privacy. Obviously, we must not allow our judgment to be swayed by the bare fact of a trend running counter to some of our traditional conventions of respect for human personality. We must be willing to take responsibility for condemning the changes that have nothing to recommend them but that they are at the least momentary successes. But is there, after all, any justification for the emphasis which in the Anglo-American tradition we have put on respect for privacy?

Let us be careful to separate the enduring values from the specific practices by which we seek to express and conserve the values. The etiquette of upper or middle class Englishmen or Americans, or even the legal arrangements evolved in the course of Anglo-American history, may not be the social forms most adequate to the full realization of the values of human dignity which are at stake.

Our overmastering goal in interpersonal relationships may, I think, be stated in terms of human dignity. I affirm my own goal values in these terms, and conceive of the task of man as guiding the processes of society toward the realization of human dignity on the world scale in theory and in fact. Among the component values designated by the term, "human dignity," I understand the sharing of respect and affection. Respect is the deference that we give and deserve in our capacity as human beings, and on the basis of our individual merit. The presumption in favor of privacy follows from our respect for freedom of choice, for autonomy, for self-direction on the part of everyone. It is apparent, of course, that the presumption on behalf of privacy is refutable when the group, by democratic processes, decides that privacy is being used in ways that result in the infliction of damage upon the members of the group (including the individuals immediately involved), or when the group decides that an emergency exists in which the activities which are necessary to the survival of the whole, no longer admit of the accustomed forms of privacy.

However, we must insist that the fact that a group decision is arrived at on a democratic basis (by a shared power process) does not in our eyes legitimatize every intrusion upon privacy. There must be an emergency. There must be strong evidence that what goes on within the customary zones of privacy culminates in acts which are genuinely damaging, such as the detailed plotting of assassination and sabotage. Otherwise the community, even though it acts as a democracy, is transgressing the respect to which everyone is entitled. (I leave to one side the next question, which is whether the individual is justified in civil disobedience in these circumstances or the use of stronger measures. At the moment my purpose is only to clarify the recommended meaning of the respect value and its relationship to privacy.)

My position is that respect for privacy is a necessary part of respect, as one of the values comprising human dignity. I think also that privacy is involved in affection and intimacy. In the commonwealth of free men we want human beings to be bound by mutual ties of affection. But the conception of shared affection does not signify that all individuals must be equally loved. On the contrary, we assume that love will be of varying intensity and expressed in various degrees of sought and granted intimacy. Hence some social conventions of privacy are components of the pattern of the relationship appropriate to shared affection.

Furthermore, I believe that privacy is a significant part of the practices involved in the sharing of other values. Consider the acquisition and exercise of many skills of artistic, philosophic, and scientific expression. Great originality is often rooted in the maturing and application of talent outside the spotlight of instant disclosure. There is a natural privacy of the gifted mind, whether in mathematical, musical, or other modes of symbolic expression. It is socially contributory to allow much leeway in private preoccupation to the gifted.

I have already said that privacy is part of respect and affection, and that it is a contributor to the useful exercise of skill. At the moment I shall add but one other point. The conception of rectitude that is appropriate to a free society, is one in which each individual shares a sense of responsibility for realizing and defending the values and institutions of freedom. In a perfectly integrated society, I suppose we can say that the individual sense of responsibility is so frequently supported by the prevailing patterns of community, that it requires no great effort on the part of the individual. Our world, however, is confronted with clashing values, as well as conflicting institutional solutions. We need men and women who have sought and found a deeply rooted system of belief in human dignity, and who have acquired a disciplined sense of responsibility for so acting, as to bring into existence the valued modes of human relationship. Such decisive figures in our turbulent epoch are almost certain to acquire much of their firmness on the basis of inner struggle. They have sought to put their minds and consciousness in harmony, and they have often done this in defiance of many of the prevailing standards of the environment in which they were brought up. The capacity to endure opprobrium, or worse, with serenity, is often the fruit of privacy, not as an end in itself—or as a means of spurning human association—but rather as a means of obtaining deeper insight.

These are some of the considerations which lead me to adhere to the conception that privacy is an integral part of a comprehensive conception of human dignity. And I might add, the traditional idea that the adherence to zones of privacy is a safeguard of democratic government.

I have already stated that one of the major threats in our time to the perpetuation of respect for privacy, is to be found in the fear on the part of democratic peoples of the external threat that comes from a Soviet bloc of garrison-police states. And I remind the reader again of the danger that in the act of preparing to avert a foreign threat to our security we subtly transform ourselves into the image of our enemy. Secret surveillance puts a dreadful weapon in the hands of government, and more especially of the agency concerned with the political police function. From the history of the Star Chamber, and of other episodes in our Anglo-American tradition, we have a lively sense of the danger of abuse that accompanies official invasions of privacy.

Having affirmed in substance the traditional view of the worth of privacy, I want to be no less categorical in acknowledging some of the adverse results of privacy. I shall do this because I propose to criticize the specific patterns of privacy that have been part of the upper and middle class tradition in the Anglo-American world.

When privacy is a byproduct of non-identification, it is a menace to many individuals who may be driven to suicide or to other acts of self-aggression. When privacy is the result of the tensions of choice, privacy often signifies the defeat of the individual in taking responsibility for himself. When privacy is the outcome of towering ambition, it is more than a threat to the deeper gratifications of the ambitious individual. It transforms human relations into a streamlined version of Hobbesian nature, in which every man's hand is swayed to the purpose of every other. The outcome of unbridled ambition is to accelerate the very process that contributes to the growth of new cases of non-identification. Great ambition is a removal from identification, a denial of the restraining components of the self in checking the aggrandizement of the primary ego.

I welcome many of the institutional devices now in the course of development for the overcoming of destructive incentives to privacy. I think it is a healthy sign that small groups are forming throughout this country for the sake of gaining insight into the self, not in isolation, but as a part of a common direct experience. This is the positive virtue of group psychotherapy, and of group manifestations of the counseling movement. Within the designative symbols provided by modern clinical psychology, human beings are rediscovering the gratifications of controlled spontaneity in human affairs. In the intimacy of the therapeutic group human beings learn of the generality, if not the universality of many of their secret burdens. Furthermore, they gain insight into the motivations which make various forms of conduct comprehensible. And this lays the foundation for the spread of common perspective on the basis of which the members of modern civilization may once again feel at home in the world.

It would be desirable for the present transition toward "the world village" to be accomplished on a voluntary basis, by the multiplication of small groups intent upon helping one another to deeper understanding through insight. But I have already called attention to the peremptory invasions of privacy that are occurring, as a result of the expansion of our new scientific and technical devices, and of the new incentives to make use of these instruments for the destruction of privacy. Under these circumstances, the "organic" process of recapturing spontaneity is likely to be interrupted, if not altogether done away entirely, leading to new excesses of privatization.

Under the diverse circumstances of modern urban civilization, people have grown away from one another in many spheres of human experience and practice. We are uncertain about the inner motivations of others, when they perform acts which, though repugnant, are, nevertheless, comprehensible, and perhaps permissible under special circumstances. One of the most arresting examples of how far we have come from common understanding, is the excitement aroused by Dr. Kinsey's report on sexual practices indulged by the American male. In one of the most discerning reviews of this report, Lionel Trilling made a crucial point. He spoke of the alienation of men from one another in our civilization, and labeled the report as a substitute for the kind of gossip and clandestine observation that establishes the structure of expectations which prevail in villages or in the life of small tribes.

If there is a sudden increase in surveillance and in the use of information about unconventional conduct as part of the criteria of personnel selection, or of extortion and blackmail, we can easily foresee some of the consequences. The crisis conditions now prevailing put much potentially prejudicial information into the hands of the political police. Even under ordinary circumstances there is fear, and withdrawal into privatization. Given the instruments of modern surveillance, these threats of deprivation are much more acute. Superficial conformism of conduct carries with it grave consequences for the individual, as well as for the psychological structure of the community taken as a whole. The gap of non-identification, to which we have referred, is widened, rather than narrowed. During the transition period, the tensions of choice are much accentuated, as new conditions (particularly new threats) are taken into account. And the tensions of ambition undergo a sharp, and even contradictory, evolution.

Egocentric personalities capable of withholding affection from

The Threat to Privacy

others, are the ones fit to survive in that sort of police state. Individuals who are more outgoing in basic personality structure are likely to make mistakes by misplaced affection, and to withdraw from competition, and to subside into bitterness and disorganization.

Knowledge about the private lives of people becomes a potent basis for power, for money, and for other values. If the garrison-police state becomes crystallized into a caste society, in which an elite of military police families and their dependents dominates the world, privacy will be denied to the rank and file of the community. It will be sought by the members of the ruling elite who desire to be protected from "scrutiny from below" and, indeed, scrutiny by one another. However, suspicions among the elite will be so intense, that we can foresee only sporadic success in the quest for privacy.

Suppose that the more revolting potentialities of the world situation do not materialize, and that it is possible to resume the march toward worldwide cooperation, this is one hope that sustains us all. But in the meanwhile we must reaffirm the positive worth of the presumptions in favor of privacy, and sustain an atmosphere in which sacrifices of privacy are kept at the minimum compatible with the security necessities of the times. And this means that we seek persons as leaders and responsible representatives, who are devoted to our fundamental values, and who are unwilling to give them up, unless a very strong case has been made for doing so in the concrete instance.

In this way the respect for privacy becomes part of the larger struggle for the protection and for the realization of human dignity in our and in future time.

[It is interesting to have this subject included in our list, because it is very definitely one of the great problems of our times.

I would like to suggest that this page can most excellently furnish much material for discussion. I would like, for example, to go beyond the notion of human dignity as a basis of certain types of privacy.

Everything that grows first of all does so in the darkness before it sends its shoots out into the light. In other words, it is a creative stage, which is part of the privacy which means the integrity of individuals.

Moreover, there is another point there, I think, where we might distinguish between the inquisitorial invasion of privacy and those other aspects of the subject which were so excellently brought forward by Professor Lasswell. In other words, if we do that, we will probably all come to the same kind of conclusion as he came to, that there is a very pressing area of human life here that is greatly in danger and one of the great problems of our time. The editor.]

CONTRIBUTORS TO "CONFLICT OF LOYALTIES"

ROGER N. BALDWIN, A.M., *Harvard University*, Chairman, National Committee, American Civil Liberties Union; Board Chairman, International League for Rights of Man; Author: (with Bernard Flexner) *Juvenile Courts and Probation, Liberty Under the Soviets;* also various pamphlets on civil liberties.

LYMAN BRYSON, LL.D., L.H.D., Professor of Education, Teachers College, Columbia University; Member, Executive Committee, The Institute for Religious and Social Studies; Member, Board of Directors, Conference on Science, Philosophy and Religion; Author: *Science and Freedom,* and others; Editor: *The Communication of Ideas;* Coeditor: Symposia of Conference on Science, Philosophy and Religion.

LOUIS FINKELSTEIN, Ph.D., *Columbia University,* Rabbi, *Jewish Theological Seminary;* President and Solomon Schechter Professor of Theology, The Jewish Theological Seminary of America; Director, The Institute for Religious and Social Studies; President, Conference on Science, Philosophy and Religion; Author: *Akiba, The Pharisees,* and others; Editor: *American Spiritual Autobiographies,* Symposia of Conference on Science, Philosophy and Religion.

F. ERNEST JOHNSON, D.D., *Albion,* Professor Emeritus of Education, Teachers College, Columbia University; Executive Director, Central Department of Research and Survey, and Editor, "Information Service," National Council of Churches of Christ in the United States of America; Author: *The Social Gospel Reexamined;* Editor: *World Order, Its Intellectual and Cultural Foundations, Foundations of Democracy, Wellsprings of the American Spirit,* and others.

HAROLD D. LASSWELL, Ph.D., *The University of Chicago,* Professor of Law, School of Law, Yale University; Member, Board of Directors, Conference on Science, Philosophy and Religion; Author: *Democracy Through Public Opinion, Politics Faces Economics, Power and Per-*

sonality, The Language of Politics, The Analysis of Political Behaviour, National Security and Individual Freedom, and others.

R. M. MacIver, D.Phil., *Edinburgh University,* D.Litt., *Columbia University, Harvard University,* Lieber Professor Emeritus of Political Philosophy and Sociology, Columbia University; Member, Executive Committee, The Institute for Religious and Social Studies; Member, Board of Directors, Conference on Science, Philosophy and Religion; Author: *Community—A Sociological Study, The Modern State, Society—Its Structure and Changes, Leviathan and the People, Social Causation, Toward an Abiding Peace, The Web of Government, The More Perfect Union;* Editor: *Group Relations and Group Antagonisms, Civilization and Group Relationships, Unity and Difference in American Life, Discrimination and National Welfare, Great Expressions of Human Rights;* Co-editor: Symposia of Conference on Science, Philosophy and Religion.

Franz L. Neumann, Ph.D., *London School of Economics and Political Science,* Professor of Government, Columbia University.

Liston Pope, Ph.D., *Yale University,* S.T.D., *Boston University,* Dean, Yale Divinity School; Author: *Millhands and Preachers;* Editor: *Labor's Relation to Church and Community.*

Robert Saudek, A.B., *Harvard University,* Vice President, American Broadcasting Company, Inc.

Hans Simons, Dr. jur. et. rer. pol., *Koenigsberg,* President, The New School for Social Research.

Ordway Tead, LL.D., *Saint Lawrence University,* LL.D., *Keuka College,* L.H.D., *Amherst College,* Chairman, Board of Higher Education of New York City; Fellow, Conference on Science, Philosophy and Religion; Author: *The Art of Administration, The Case for Democracy, New Adventures in Democracy, Democratic Administration, Equalizing Educational Opportunities Beyond the Secondary School,* and others; Co-author: *Modern Education and Human Values, College Teaching and College Learning.*

W. W. Waymack, D.Sc., *Iowa State College,* etc., former member, United States Atomic Energy Commission.

INDEX

Abel, Theodore, 10
Acheson, Dean, 63, 64
"Acres of Diamonds," 71
Acton, Lord, on power, 60
Aged, the, 59
Aggression:
　in Germany, 10
　warlike, 91
Alliances:
　dubious, 62-67
　with governments, 64
Ambition:
　characteristic of, 116
　stress and strain of, 133-134
　unbridled, 137
American Civil Liberties Union, 37
American culture, values in, 69-72
Anomie, problem of, 132
Anthropologists, cultural, 33
Anti-Communism, 63
Antigone, tragedy of, 1-7
Antioch Review, 59
Anxiety, uncertainty and, 132
Apostles' Creed, 34
Appropriateness, 67
Aptitude tests, 127
Aquinas, St. Thomas, 47
Arcana doctrines, 48
Aristotle, 1, 46
Arnold, Benedict, 118
Assassination, 45-49
Assemblage, peaceful, 38, 39
Atomic bomb, 62, 78-88
Atomic energy, program for control of, 80
Attitudes:
　maintaining, 59-62
　status quo, 63
Augustine, Saint, 47
Aurelius, Marcus, quoted, 77
Axiological world, 30

Baeck, Leo, 94
Baldwin, Roger N., 37, 141
Bill of Rights, 84
Birth control, 59
Blackmail, 138
Boucher, Jean, 49
Brightman, Edgar S., 100
Britain:
　and India, 15
　democracy in, 14, 63
　empire and democracy, 14
　likened to Romans, 15
　nineteenth-century, 21
Brotherhood of man, 88
Brutus, Junius, 49
Bryson, Lyman, 9, 94, 141
Business man, American, 69

Calvin, John, 48
Calvinism, 49
Camera, modern, 125, 126
Candid camera, 126
Capitalism, 70
Capitalists, 62, 63
Carnegie, Dale, 72
Censorship, educational, 99-112
Census, and privacy, 124
China, urbanity, a ritual in, 27
Choice, tensions of, 132-133
City manager, 11-12
Civil liberties, essence of, 37
Civil Liberties Union, American, 37
Civil litigation, privacy in, 123-124
Civil rights, Jehovah's Witnesses and, 39-42
Civil war, 62
Clan, 89-90
Class, privacy and, 122
Classless society, 61

Index

Clearchus, assassination of, 46
Coercion, 123
  freedom and, 52
Cold war, 80
College education, 101-102
Colleges and universities:
  boards and trustees, 104-105
  federal influence, 107-108
  psychological considerations, 108-110
  state influence, 107
  trustees, 110
Communications:
  mass, 113-119
  newspapers, 116-117
  radio, 118
  television, 118
Communism, 70
  philosophy of, 84
Communist party, teacher members of, 107
Communists, 131
Compromise:
  for a cause, 60
  for self-preservation, 59
Compulsion, in place of conflict, 118-119
Compunctions, 83-84
Conflict, compulsion in place of, 118-119
Conformity, and freedom, 61
Conscientious objectors, 37, 38
  Jehovah's Witnesses, 41
Constitution of State of Hessen, Germany, 50-51
Conwell, Russell H., 71
Copernican revolution, 86
Corporation, a legal fiction, 34
Council of Constance, 48
Council of Paris, 47
Counseling movement, 137
Creed, 34-35
Crime:
  and privacy of individual, 123
  as national issue, 130
Crito, 5
Croker, Richard, 117
Cultural achievements:
  French, 20
  German, 20
  power not justified by, 19

Cultural anthropologists, 33
Custom, value of, 5-6
Cynic, definition of, 70
Cynicism, institutions founded on, 17-18

Death sentence, 57, 58
Decisions, group, 135
Declaration of Independence, 50
Democracy, 11, 12
  and expansion, 61
  Britain, 14, 63
  end of, 12
  Greece, 14
  leader in, 13
  purpose of, 12
  United States, 63-64
Democracy's College, 107
Democratic society, conflicts in, 115
Democratic theories, justifiable disobedience, 50, 53
Denominationalism, 98
Denominations, loyalty to own, 94
Depression, war and, 58
Detective agencies, private, 129
Dialectical materialism, 84, 86
Dickinson, John, 4-5
Dictatorship of the proletariat, 61
Dickhoff, John, 107
Differences of background, 97
Dignity, human, 134, 135, 136
Disobedience, justifiable (*see* Justifiable disobedience)
Dissent, 37-43
Distrust, worldwide, 66
Diversity, principle of, 87
Drugs, 125, 126

Economic motives, 69-72
Economics, and our moral history, 114
Education:
  and general public, 111
  boards of trustees, colleges and universities, 104-105
  budget retrenchment in, 102
  citizen responsibility for, 109-110
  freedom and interference in, 99-112
  higher (*see* Colleges and universities)
  liberal arts, 101

Index

Education (*cont.*):
  loyalty oaths, 107
  patriotic societies 105-106
  professional associations, 104
  required specified subjects, 104
  ROTC and, 107
  school boards, 103, 110
  school budgets, 103
  secularization of, 102
  special interest groups, 105-106
  state boards, 103
  state superintendent, 103
  teachers (*see* Teachers)
  textbooks, 105-106
  too much for too many, 101-102
  vocational, 101
  voluntary accrediting agency, 104
Educational institutions, and development of better men, 91
Educationalists, differences of approach, 101
Einstein, Albert, 29
Electronic media, 118
Emancipation, 38
Emergencies, privacy and, 134-135
Empire building, 13
  purpose of, 15
Ends, and means, 57-67
England, Elizabethan, 20
Englishmen, traditional rights of, 129
Enmity between groups, 61-62
Equality, 33-34
  racial, 33
Equilibrium, 87
Ethical realities, 26
Euthanasia, 57
Evolution of Physics, The, 29

Facts:
  manipulation of, 28
  objectivity in reporting, 33
Family, 89-90
Fascists, 131
Federal control, colleges and universities, 107-108
Fermi, Enrico, 77
Fiction, 26
  corporation a legal, 34

Fifth columns, 64
Finkelstein, Louis, 89, 141
Flag salute, 38
France, 20
Francis of Assisi, Saint, 75
François-Hotman, 49
Frank, Judge Jerome N., 30, 31
Frankness, perfect, 26
Freedom:
  and conformity, 61
  closed theories of, 13
  coercion and, 52
  definition of, 53
  Kant on, 51-52
  of press, 117, 127
  of thought, 16, 37
  open theory of, 13, 16
  through compromise, 59-60
Free enterprise system, 101
French, likened to Greeks, 15
Fromm, Erich, 132
Frontier, and American development, 114, 129-130
Fugitive slave law, 38
Fusion bombs, 79

Gabriel, Ralph, 71
Gadget approach to techniques, 60
Gadgets, 89
Gandhi, Mahatma, 38
Gangsterism, 130
Garrison-police state, 136
  egocentric individuals in, 138-139
Genesis, Book of, 90, 93
Genghis Khan, 82
Germans, reaction to Hitler, 10
Germany:
  and death sentence, 57
  between Bismarck and Hitler, 20
  Hitler's leadership of, 10
  rearmament in, 65-66
  women from, 11-12
Gibson, W. W., 70
Gifted mind, privacy and, 133, 135
Glass, one-way, 125
Goodman, Christopher, 49
"Gotham," 70
Greece, Periclean, 20

Greeks:
  democracy of, 14
  French likened to, 15
Group decisions, 135
Group psychotherapy, 137
Guilds, 91
Guilt feelings, 114

Hamlet, tragedy of, 1
Hand, Judge Learned, 30
Hauser, Gaylord, 114
Health services, 58
Hegel, Georg W. F., 54, 56
  on Antigone, 4
Hessian constitution, 50-51
Hipparchus, assassination of, 45-46
Hiroshima, 77-88
Hitler, Adolf, 10, 94
  attempt on life of, 46
Hobbes, Thomas, 52
Holmes, Justice Oliver Wendell, 30
Honesty, 33
Hood, Robin, 72
Horizontal mobility, and privacy, 129-130, 131
Human dignity, 134, 135, 136
Human nature, no need to transform, 93
Human relations, and equilibrium, 87
Hume, David, 54
Hypnosis, 125

Idealists, social, 33
Imperialism, 91
Imperialists, Western, 62
Imposition, method of, 60-61
India:
  aid to, 65
  Britain and, 15
Industrial Workers of the World, 39, 40
Infield, Leopold, 29
Inner voice, 56
Inquiry, free, 15
Inquisition, the, 38
Institutes, Calvin, 48
Institutionalism:
  and faith, 89-98
  evils of, 91-92
  loyalty to title or name, 91-92

Institutions:
  danger and promise, 89
  family or clan, 89-90
  founded on cynicism, 17-18
  in urban life, 90-91
  religious, 92-98
International Bible Students Association, 40
Interpersonal relationships, goal in, 134
Iron Curtain, 85
Isolation, "splendid," 133
I.W.W., 39, 40

James, Jesse, 118
James, William, 90
Japan, atomic warfare in, 77-88
Jefferson, Thomas, 38
Jehovah's Witnesses, 39-42, 43
Jeremiah, 96, 97
Jesus, quoted, 69
Jewish Theological Seminary, The, 95
John of Salisbury, 47
Johnson, F. Ernest, 25, 141
Jury, trial by, 30-31
Justice, 33
Justifiable disobedience, 37-43
  democratic theories, 50, 53
  functional theory, 49-50
  historical survey, 45-49
  limits of, 45-56
  natural law theories, 50, 51-52, 54
  when permissible, 49-55

Kant, Immanuel, 16, 53
  on freedom, 51-52
Kinsey, Dr., 43, 138
Korean war, 59

Labor:
  fight for rights, 39
  management and, 91
Lasswell, Harold D., 93, 121, 141
Law:
  affecting life and liberty, 55, 56
  behind law, 6
  obedience to, 37-43
  of the land, 6
  positive, 50
  retroactive, 55

Index

Lawbreakers, moral, 37-43
Leader:
  as teacher, 16-17
  chief work of, 18
  deception by, 9-23
  function of, 9
  in democracy, 13
  license given to, 19
  of free country, 11
  temptation of, 9
Legal code, 6
Liberal arts education, 101
Lie detection, 125, 128
Life expectancy, extension of, 59
Light, phenomena of, 29-30
Lincoln, Abraham, 33, 82, 118
Literalism, moral, 26
Lloyd George, David, 27-28
Locke, John, 52
Look Younger, Live Longer, 114
Louis, Duke of Orléans, 47
Loyalties, narrow *v.* wide, 63
Loyalty oaths, 38, 107
Loyalty program, 128
Luke, Gospel of, 69, 72-74
Luther, Martin, 48
Lying:
  inhibition against, 26
  right or wrong, 6-7

Machiavelli, 6, 114
MacIver, R. M., 1, 142
Major Barbara, 113
Mammon of unrighteousness, 69-75
Man:
  an economic being, 71
  reorientation of, who shall undertake, 93
Management, and labor, 91
Mariana, Juan de, 49
Martyrs, 59, 93-94
Marxism, 66
Mass communication, 113-119
Mass destruction in war, 82
Materialism, dialectical, 84, 86
Means:
  ends and, 58-67
  men as, 16

Means (*cont.*):
  morality of, 84-85
Men, as means or as ends, 16
Men Who Control Our Universities, 104
Microphones, concealed, 125, 128-129
Millionaires, 69
Momism, 114
Montague, William P., 35
Moral law, 5
Moral lawbreakers, 37-43
Morals, and methods, 84
Myth, 26
  religious, 35
  use of term, 34

Nagasaki, 79, 82
Name, loyalty to, 91-92
National security, and invasion of privacy, 128
National Socialism, 59, 131
Nations, individual, different goals in, 18-19
Natural law, 50, 51-52, 54
Natural law theories, justifiable disobedience, 50, 51-52, 54
Natural right, 50
Nazis, 59, 131
Neumann, Franz L., 45, 142
Newspapers:
  government-owned, 116-117
  reporters, and sources of information, 124
Newtonian discoveries, 86
New York State, Board of Regents, 103
Nuclear weapons, 62, 78-88

Obedience to law, 37-43
Oedipus, tragedy of, 1, 2
Orestes, tragedy of, 1
Organized religion, Jehovah's Witnesses and, 42

Patriotic societies, and education, 105-106
Peace, 85
Peaceful assemblage, 38, 39
Pearl Harbor, 85
Personnel selection, 127, 138
Petit, Jean, 47, 48

Index

Picketing, 38
Plato, 5, 22, 46
Platonism, 55
Point IV program, 70
Police state (*see* Garrison-police state)
Policraticus, 47
Political action, purpose of, 12
Political murder, 48
Political myths, founded on facts, 14-15
Political Science Quarterly, 4
Poltrot, Jean de, 49
Polygamy, 42
Pope, Liston, 69, 142
Positive law, 50
Power:
  and cultural achievements, 19
  Lord Acton on, 60
Poynet, John, 49
Prejudice, 33
President's Commission on Higher Education, Report of, 107
Preventive war, 85
Privacy:
  adverse results of, 137-139
  and class, 122
  and frontier, 129-130
  and human dignity, 134, 135, 136
  and occupation, 122
  Anglo-American respect for, 121-122, 134, 137
  animosity against, 133-134
  confessional relationship and, 124
  emergencies and, 134-135
  enforced disclosure and, 125-126
  formal, 123
  informal, 121-122
  legal doctrines and observances, 123-126
  litigation granted, 124
  national security and, 128
  of gifted mind, 133, 135
  of thought, 133
  originality and, 135
  outcome of ambition, 137
  professional relationship and, 124
  tests, psychiatric appraisals and, 127
  threat to, 121-140
  urbanization and, 138

Professional groups, 90
Professional persons, conflicting loyalties of, 6
Progressive education, 101
Prohibition era, 32, 38, 43, 130
Proletariat, dictatorship of, 61
Propaganda, bad, essence of, 32-33
Psychiatric appraisals, 127
Psychiatry, 114
Psychic isolation, 132
Psychotherapy, group, 137
Public, deception for good of, 9-23
Purgatory, 57

Race relations, 33
Racketeers, 130
Radioactivity, 78, 79
Radio law, 118
Reality, contradictory pictures of, 29, 30
Rearmament, German, 65-66
Regicide, 45-46, 49
  doctrines, 47-48
Relativity, concept of, 29, 86-87
Religion, organized, Jehovah's Witnesses and, 42
Religious creeds, 34-35
Religious institutions, 92-98
  deification of, 93
  groups in, 94
Religious myths, 35
Republic, Plato's, 46
Resistance, right of, 45-56
Retroactive laws, 55
Revolution, 62
  Jefferson on, 38
Right, meaning of term, 50, 51
Rights:
  natural, 50, 51-52, 54
  unconditional, of resistance, 55-56
Rockefeller, John D., Sr., 71
Romans, as empire builders, 14
Roosevelt, Theodore, 22
ROTC, and education, 107
Rousseau, Jean Jacques, 53, 54
Rulers:
  Machiavelli on, 6
  regicide, 45-46, 49
Russell, Pastor, 40

Russelites (*see* Jehovah's Witnesses)
Russia (*see* Soviet Russia)

Sanctions, 23
Saudek, Robert, 113, 142
Schechter, Solomon, 95
School boards, local, 103, 110
School groups, 90
Schools (*see* Education)
Science of today, 29
Sects, loyalty to own, 94
Secularization in education, 102
Security act, 62
Self-centeredness, material strength and, 65
Self-preservation, compromising for, 59
Shaw, George Bernard, 113
Simons, Hans, 57, 142
Slogans, founded on fact, 14-15
Slyness, characteristic of, 116
Smith, T. V., 34
Social climbing, 133
Social idealists, 33
Social science courses, 106
Society, type desired, 13
Socrates, 5
Sorel, Georges, 54
Sovereignty, Dickinson on, 5
Soviet Russia, 17-18
    and respect for privacy, 136
    death sentence in, 58
    enmity toward others, 61-62
    means and ends, 61
    policy of, 66
Special interest groups, in education, 105-106
Spinoza, Baruch, 52
Star chamber, 136
State controls, colleges and universities, 107
Status, appraisal of, 69-70
Status quo attitude, 63
Steward, unjust, parable of, 72-74
Story of the Other Wise Man, 28-29
Strength:
    material, 65
    moral, 65
Student-centered education, 101

Subject-centered education, 101
Submarine, 81, 82
Suicide, in modern nations, 132
Superiority feelings, 60-61
Supreme Court, United States, 37
    Jehovah's Witnesses, cases before, 40-42

Taft, Chief Justice William Howard, 30
Teachers:
    criticism of, 106
    freedom of utterance, 106-107, 111, 112
    leader as, 16-17
    "leftist," 106
    membership in Communist party, 107
    representation on trustee bodies, 110-111
    respect for contemporary knowledge of, 110
Tead, Ordway, 99, 142
Teams, baseball or football, 90-91
Tea Pot Dome scandal, 117
Telephone tap, 125, 128-129
Television, 118
Temperament tests, 127
Ten Commandments, 29
Tests, and privacy, 127
Textbooks, 105-106
Third degree, 128
Thomistic system, 51
Thoreau, Henry, 38
Title, loyalty to, 91-92
Totalitarian countries, freedom in, 13
Trade unions, 90
Traditional education, 101
Traitors, successful, 38
Trials:
    by jury, 30-31
    war crimes, 58
Tribal organizations, 90
Trilling, Lionel, 138
Trustees, college or university, 204-205
    faculty representation, 110-111
Truth, vital, communication of, 36
Truthfulness:
    differentiated from factual exactness, 26
    honored position of, 25, 26

Truth-*versus*-fact dilemma, 29
Turner, Frederick Jackson, 114
Tweed Ring, 117
Tyrannicide, 45-49
Tyrants, 12
  assassination of, 45-49
  most dangerous, 18
  types of, 46

Uncertainty, and anxiety, 132
Unemployment, war and, 58
United Nations, 95
United States:
  as vast village, 131
  "open ego" in, 122
  atomic energy control program, 80
Unity, principle of, 87
Universalism, 55
Universities, state, political influence in, 107 (*see also* Colleges and universities)
Unselfishness, 33
Urban life:
  and privacy, 138
  institutions in, 90-91
Urbanity, 26
  in China, 27

Values:
  in American culture, 69-72
  world of, 30
Van Dyke, Henry, 28

Village:
  United States as, 131
  world as, 93, 137
V-mail, 131
Vocational education, 101
Voice of America, 64
Voluntary accrediting agency, 104
Voluntary organizations, 90-91

War:
  arguments for, 58
  conscientious objectors, 38
  modern, 81-85
  moral equivalent for, 90
  preventive, 85
War crimes trials, 58
Warmongers, 62
Washington, George, 118
Waste, social, 32
Waymack, W. W., 77, 142
Wealth, gospel of, 71, 72
Weapons, atomic, 62, 78-88
Weimar Republic, 51
Wesley, John, 71
White man's burden, 23
Wilde, Oscar, 70
Wiretapping, 125, 128-129
Woman preacher, story of, 28
Woodbridge, Professor, 35-36
World village, 93, 137
World War I:
  destruction of commerce, 82
  returned soldiers, 131
World War II, returned soldiers, 131-132